RAOUL'S TREASURE

Arriving in Bradley Creek, Jack
Strother defends an old man and
is pitched into a confrontation with
Ben Bradley, the region's biggest
rancher. Now an enemy of Bradley,
Strother leaves town, but is forced
to return on learning that the old
man is dying and wishes to pass on
something. But what he gives
Strother leads him to a mountain of
trouble near the Mexican border.
Will the future be no more than a
grave in the desert?

SKEETER DODDS

RAOUL'S TREASURE

Complete and Unabridged

LINFORD
Leicester

First published in Great Britain in 2005 by
Robert Hale Limited
London

First Linford Edition
published 2006
by arrangement with
Robert Hale Limited
London

British Library CIP Data

Dodds, Skeeter
　　Raoul's treasure.—Large print ed.—
Linford western library
1. Western stories
2. Large type books
I. Title
823.9'2 [F]

ISBN 1–84617–547–X

Published by
F. A. Thorpe (Publishing)
Anstey, Leicestershire

Set by Words & Graphics Ltd.
Anstey, Leicestershire
Printed and bound in Great Britain by
T. J. International Ltd., Padstow, Cornwall

This book is printed on acid-free paper

1

'Let the old-timer be!'

Jack Strother's whiplike command had the two men obstructing the old man's progress along the boardwalk spinning round. The younger of the duo, liquor-flushed and mean of spirit, glared at Strother with blue eyes that could be friendly, if the man was not so full of anger and spite. However, Strother reckoned that they had long ago been poisoned by the man's bad-tempered nature. The younger man pushed back his hat from his sweating forehead and a bunch of fair hair poked from under its brim. He wiped the sweat from his face, generated by the liquor sloshing in his belly, his blue eyes locking with Strother's slate grey stare.

'Is it any business of yours what me and Joe get up to, mister?' he snarled.

'Ain't no bother to me.' The old-timer laughed nervously. 'These fine young fellas are just funning round, mister. Ain't that so, boys?'

The old-timer was quaking. That told Jack Strother that the gents he had rebuked were well-known for their mean nature, and that the old man feared a comeback when he was not around. It settled gallishly with Strother that he should withdraw his objection to the bullying behaviour, but he could understand the old-timer's trepidation. A short stay to get supplies and sup a little whiskey, and he'd be on his way out of Bradley Creek. He yielded to the plea in the old-timer's watery eyes.

'If you say so, old-timer,' he said.

'Sure do, mister,' the old man croaked, relieved.

He went to get by, but the man called Joe blocked the old-timer's path.

'Didn't I tell you to get out of town yesterday?' he growled.

'No, sir. Not me, you didn't.'

Joe addressed his partner. 'He's lying. I told him, Ben. The old fool bumped against me in the saloon and spilled my liquor.'

'I just arrived in town, mister,' the old man asserted.

'Then you must have a double,' Joe barked.

'And where the hell do you think you're going?' the man called Ben questioned Jack Strother.

Strother replied frostily: 'About my business. Not that what I do is any of your damn affair.'

'You know who you're talking to?' Ben enquired of Strother. 'Reckon you don't,' was his raised eyebrow conclusion.

'I can go round.' The old-timer pointed back along the street, indicating another route to his destination. 'Makes no diff'rence to me how I reach the gen'ral store, mister.'

'You stay put, old-timer,' Joe growled. 'Mr Bradley ain't finished with you yet, you lying old bastard.'

A man came hurrying along the boardwalk wearing a star.

'What seems to be the trouble, Ben?' he enquired. The friendliness of his address told Jack Strother that instead of two, he was now facing three.

'This stranger is poking his nose in where it's got no business to be, Sam,' Ben told the marshal.

The lawman snorted, his heavy black eyebrows coming together.

'That a fact.' It was a statement, not a question. 'Guess he don't know who you are, Ben.'

'I don't care who he is,' Strother said stonily. 'But whoever he is, Marshal, he's got the manners of a damn hog and the attitude of a fool. A mighty dangerous combination, I'd say.'

Not used to be being put in his place, Ben Bradley's jaw dropped, and his sidekick's eyes popped. And the marshal would rather be anywhere else. The old-timer had the hint of a smile playing on his lips. When Bradley recovered, he barked:

'I ain't going to stand for that kind of lip!'

'You apologize to Mr Bradley right now, mister,' the marshal demanded. 'Or I'll sling you in the caboose 'til you rot!'

The picture was becoming clearer for Jack Strother. Ben's name was Bradley. He was in a town called Bradley Creek. And everyone, including the law, kowtowed to him. The big man of the area, he reckoned.

'Did you hear the marshal?' Ben rasped, when Strother didn't lick his boots.

'I heard, Bradley.'

'That'll be *Mr* Bradley!'

'Respect has to be earned, friend,' Strother opined. 'And you're a long way off deserving it.'

Ben Bradley's face became mottled with rage. His words choked in his throat. The marshal stepped in.

'You're going to jail, fella.'

Jack Strother took a couple of paces back.

5

'I've done nothing to go to jail for, Marshal.' His tone was hollow. 'All the wrong is on Bradley's side.'

A crowd had gathered to witness the rare event in Bradley Creek of someone standing up to Ben Bradley and Marshal Sam Cranton, Bradley's protector and lackey. But now the crowd separated, leaving a clear line of fire should a gunfight between the marshal and the bold stranger erupt.

Along the street a woman whom God had favoured bountifully in beauty and form paused as she left the hotel, her interest given over to the stand-off outside the saloon.

'Marshal, this impasse can be easily solved by Bradley and his cohort showing courtesy to the old-timer,' Jack Strother said. 'Just let him pass, and this is done and dusted.'

The lawman looked hopefully at Bradley.

'This ain't about the old man any more, Cranton,' he glowered.

'Let the old-timer pass, Joe,' Bradley

ordered his sidekick.

Joe stepped aside.

Passing Jack Strother, the old man murmured:

'I thank you, mister. But I surely don't want you to get killed because of me. There's three of them.'

'You go about your business,' Strother said kindly. 'I got into this freely.'

Looking pained, the old-timer hurried away.

'Now, mister,' Bradley shifted his stance and spread his legs, his hands hovering over the twin pearl-handled Colts he wore, 'let's settle this.'

Words once spoken to him by an old lawman, every minute as old as the old-timer he had helped, came winging back to Strother.

'*Most times, fancy guns don't make for fancy shootin'.*'

Jack Strother hoped that this was one of those times. He was fast. But there was always someone faster. And that someone was almost always encountered in a burg of no great importance like Bradley Creek. Strother figured that Ben Bradley was the kind of man who would prefer to get in some shooting practice than bed a woman, because killing was his real passion.

'Now, Ben — '

'Shuddup, Cranton,' Bradley bellowed, cutting off the marshal's attempt at reconciliation.

Strother wished now that he had listened to his first thoughts to give Bradley Creek a wide berth and go on to Willsburg, a town ten miles south, before breaking his journey. But, he reckoned philosophically that in the lawless land of the West a man's life hung by a thread of fickle fate that could be cut at any moment. In the danger-filled territory he traversed it was only a fool who thought of life in days to be lived, rather than seconds to be survived.

'You know, Joe. I figure that this honcho is yella through and through,' Ben Bradley gloated. It was a view shared by his sidekick but not by the marshal who, with the wisdom of experience, could see a lot more grit in the stranger than either Bradley or his partner. If he was reading him right, and he reckoned he was, the stranger's reluctance to draw on Bradley did not stem from fear, but rather from the certain knowledge that he would kill Bradley. And killing the hothead rancher would be only the first pebble in a mountain of trouble.

'Why don't you just ride on, stranger?' Cranton suggested.

'He can't do that,' Bradley sniggered. 'Never saw a dead man sit a saddle, Sam.'

Laughing out loud, Joe obviously thought he had heard the rib-tickler of a lifetime.

'Listen to the marshal,' Jack Strother advised Bradley. 'Let this rest.'

'Not before you're wormbait, mister!' snarled Ben Bradley.

'In that case . . . ' Strother shrugged. 'Make your play.'

'Gentlemen, please.' The intervention

of the woman who had been watching from the hotel came as a surprise. 'Gunfire gives me the most dreadful headache. Isn't that so, Bambridge?' she asked the bowler-hatted man accompanying her.

'Yes, m'lady,' bowler-hat affirmed.

The elegantly clad woman and her bowler-hatted servant were now the centre of attention.

'Don't she sure talk funny,' a man in the crowd said to the man alongside him.

'Yeah,' the man agreed. 'Don't talk American proper, that's what makes her talk so darn funny, Andy.'

Andy's eyes drank in the woman's shapely form, and then, looking down in wonder, he said:

'Ya know Ned, that woman's got the power to raise the dead.'

Ned shifted sheepishly. 'Know what you mean, Andy,' he said, with a matching grin.

'Now, gentlemen,' she placated, 'why don't you buy me a drink and forget all this foolish nonsense.' She smiled and the sun faded. 'The world doesn't have that many handsome men that it can afford to lose another one of you fine gentlemen.'

She looked first at Jack Strother, who remained unimpressed by her come-hither look. She was not angry that Strother was ignoring her; she was more curious that he could. Finding Strother uncooperative, she switched her gaze to Ben Bradley, who gulped.

'It would be my pleasure to buy you a drink, ma'am,' he croaked.

Strother could see the relief flood through Sam Cranton, but he had no charitable thoughts towards the marshal. Because he figured that had he thought that Ben Bradley could have taken him, he'd have let him. The quick exchange of glances between the two men left the lawman in no doubt about how correctly Jack Strother had assessed him.

'Coming, sir?' the woman asked Strother.

'No, ma'am,' he said. 'The thirst for whiskey has gone right off me.'

'There are other desires beside whiskey,' the woman teased.

Jack Strother chuckled. 'And there's a time and place for all things, ma'am.'

'Get lost, Joe,' was Bradley's waspish command to his sidekick when he tried to shoehorn in.

Jack Strother turned and walked away. Casting a swift glance Joe's way, he saw that his humour was grim and dour. Bradley's sidekick had lost heavily and was soured in measure. He had been cheated of a gunfight, and he had also been denied a look-in with the woman.

Strother reckoned that his trouble with Joe was only beginning.

2

It would be sensible to mount up and ride on once his horse had been fed and watered, but it was late in the day and the mare was tired. Ahead of Jack Strother lay a long stretch of desert terrain that would sap both man and beast quickly, were they to start out on the journey unrested. So once he had housed the mare in the livery, Strother made his way to the hotel, hoping that its prices would be affordable. Other than the hotel, he had seen only a couple of doss-houses by way of accommodation — establishments that probably had bugs bigger than a man's fist. And where a man would be lucky, if he survived the bugs' feasting, to avoid the flash of a knife or the squeezing of a garrote. To the men who slept in the doss-houses, murder for a couple of nickels would be justified. And for a whole dollar, a man would be hanged, drawn and quartered.

The desk clerk looked up as Strother entered the hotel foyer, and was visibily shocked that the hotel might, if he had the money, have to have the dust-laden man under its roof.

Unfazed by the clerk's open disapproval, Strother enquired:

'How much are your rooms?'

'Too much, I dare say,' was the clerk's reply.

'How damn much?' Jack Strother grated.

'Two dollars a night. Hot water for washing and extra blankets cost more. And if you want to have a bath — '

'Got a town pump?' Strother interjected.

'Yes. Back of the livery.'

'That'll do.'

The bowler-hatted man who had been with the woman who had stopped the gunfight, came hurrying into the foyer and hastened upstairs.

'Funny looking duds that fella's got,'

was Strother's observation to the desk clerk, who was totally uninterested in his comments, so intense was his worry for the woman.

'I hope Lady Lyle-Hackett has come to no harm, sir,' he called.

Strother whistled. 'Lady, huh?'

'No. Good of you to ask. Her ladyship has just sent me on an errand.'

The clerk turned his attention back to Strother. 'Want a room or not?' he said, petulantly.

'I guess I do.'

'Then,' his eyes roamed over Jack Strother's dishevelled appearance, 'you will have to wash before you can lie in one of our beds.'

'That town pump will have me as clean as a newborn babe in no time at all.'

'You intend to wash in public?' the clerk asked, horrified.

'That's what I'm saying, friend.'

'But you'll be . . . '

'Buck naked?'

'Yes.'

Strother put two dollars on the desk, and held out his hand for the room key. Shocked, the clerk handed one to him.

'Thirteen, huh,' Strother said, looking at the room number. Going upstairs, he mumured: 'I sure hope that thirteen is my lucky number.' At the top of the stairs he collided with bowler-hat, hurrying back to her ladyship with a tightly held roll of dollar bills.

'My most sincere apologies, sir,' he said.

'I ran into you,' Strother pointed out.

'Still, I do beg you to forgive my clumsiness,' he pleaded.

'Consider yourself forgiven, friend,' Strother said.

'Most gracious.'

Bowler-hat hurried away.

* * *

An hour later, when the shadows were thickening, Strother made his way to the rear of the livery to the town pump, where he stripped off and began to wash. A woman passing in front of the alley that ran alongside the livery and which gave a view of the town pump, screamed on seeing Strother togged off. That was her first reaction. However, on a keen-eyed persusal, her horror turned to doe-eyed interest. Strother grabbed his clothing and disappeared into the gloom, not wanting to end up in the town gaol for indecency. And that was when the woman started to scream again, leaving Jack Strother wondering whether she was protesting or regretting. He liked to think that it was the latter, but was not prepared to hang around to find out.

As he passed the saloon on his way back to the hotel, the crowd overflowing through the batwings interested him. Normally not the curious type, he stopped to see what the commotion was all about.

'It's that fancy-talkin' woman who arrived in town today,' one of the crowd told Strother. 'Plays poker and smokes a stogie like no woman I ever seen!'

He pushed into the saloon with the crowd. The English woman was seated at a table, dealing poker with the kind of slick-fingered deal that any professional gambler would be proud of. And the fella he had enquired of in the crowd was right. She smoked a stogie like any man, chewing and puffing and rolling the smoke between her teeth with a skill that had not been learned the day before.

'I'll be damned!' Strother murmured, the admiration in his voice unmistakable.

Just then, instinctively aware of his presence, or so Strother liked to flatter himself, she turned her head.

'Perhaps you would like to join us, sir?' she invited.

'He ain't welcome,' Ben Bradley piped up.

'Nonsense,' the woman said. 'I would find the gentleman's company most enjoyable, Mr Bradley.'

'He ain't no gentleman!' Bradley growled.

The English aristocrat chuckled throatily, her eyes suggestively raking over Strother.

'How very interesting.'

Ben Bradley delivered an ultimatum, confident of its success.

'If he joins, I leave.'

The woman's jovial mood vanished instantly.

'Then leave,' she said flatly.

The relaxed and sociable mood that had permeated the saloon up to that second, was replaced by a shifting unease among the patrons.

'Are you saying that you'd prefer that toerag's company to mine?' Bradley asked, bemused.

The woman did not hesitate in her reply.

'That is what I am saying, Mr Bradley,' she stated boldly.

Rejected, and the object of intense scrutiny, Ben Bradley stood up and kicked back his chair.

'Mister,' he stated, 'I should have killed you when I had the chance. But

I'm going to kill you now.'

Jack Strother sighed. He might be getting the wrong end of the stick, but he figured that the woman, for her own amusement, had mischievously if not maliciously railroaded Ben Bradley into confronting him again.

He was not going to play her game.

'Easy, Bradley,' he said. 'I wouldn't sit in if you gave me a pot of gold.'

'A dime will do,' she said. 'Have you got that much?'

'Yes, ma'am.'

'Your ladyship,' Bambridge corrected Strother.

'If ma'am is good enough for an American woman,' Strother grated. 'It's darn well good enough for any other kind.'

'Don't trouble yourself, Bambridge,' she said, when the manservant threatened to challenge Strother. The woman pushed her considerable winnings to the centre of the table. 'It's not exactly a pot of gold, but it is a thousand dollars against your dime that Ben will outdraw you. However, I shall have to ask you to place your dime on the table.' Her smile was a taunting one. 'It would be most improper to have to search your trouser pockets for it. And I always collect a bet.'

When the collective intake of breath died away, Jack Strother answered.

'No bet.' And pointedly added: 'Ma'am.'

'You disappoint me, sir.'

Strother, annoyed by the woman's casual sacrificing of a man's life, said stonily:

'Ma'am, I think there's a rock some place that you crawled out from under, that you should crawl back under again.'

He turned to leave.

'You can't insult Lady Lyle-Hackett like that,' Bradley barked. 'Not while I'm around to protect her honour.'

'I thank you, Mr Bradley, for coming to the defence of my honour.'

'My pleasure, your ladyship,' Bradley crowed.

'Now you just tell me exactly where you want this windbag shot, your ladyship.'

'Where would you like Mr Bradley to shoot you?' she enquired of Strother, the devil's mischief dancing in her hazel eyes. 'It's most kind of Mr Bradley to be so considerate, don't you think?'

'Go to hell, ma'am!' Strother said.

'That damn woman's too cocky by a long shot,' a drunk at the bar bellowed, fumbling for his sixgun.

A black blur passed in front of Jack Strother's eyes. And it was only when the manservant's bowler-hat cleaved the drunk's head off and pitched it on to the bartop, that Strother, or for that matter anyone else in the saloon, recognized it for what it was. A silence as still as that found in a tomb fell over the saloon. Unperturbed, Lady Lyle-Hackett's manservant strode across the saloon to collect the deadly weapon. He used a bar towel to wipe the blood off the brim of the bowler.

'It has a steel brim as sharp as a

guillotine,' Lady Lyle-Hackett explained. 'Perfectly balanced. And a most efficient and entirely admirable weapon, don't you think?' she asked Strother.

Jack Strother did not offer an opinion. But he found no fault with her reasoning. It was indeed a deadly weapon in the equally deadly manservant's hands.

'I thought I had better act, m'lady,' he said. 'Before your little amusement was ruined by that drunken lout.'

'Thank you, Bambridge,' Lady Lyle-Hackett said. 'You did indeed anticipate my possible displeasure.'

Bowler hat bowed.

'Glad to be of service, m'lady.'

'I've wearied of this game,' she announced. 'I shall be away to my bed.'

Bambridge scooped up her winnings and followed her as she swept regally past Strother. He was of a mind to warn her that in the short distance to the hotel, carrying that kind of bundle could be fraught with danger. He could see that, in spite of the business that the

Bradley ranch put the town's way, Bradley Creek had a lot of out-of-work and desperate men. Lady Lyle-Hackett's poker-haul would be a terrible temptation. Bambridge could only do so much. There was nothing he could do were a flying knife to come from a dark alley. As it turned out, his urge to explain the dangers to her was pre-empted by her invitation.

'Why don't you walk me to the hotel, sir?' she said to Strother. 'As a back-up to Bambridge, should anyone attempt to relieve me of my winnings. Would a hundred dollars be sufficient to engage your services?'

Jack Strother was of a mind to deliver a spirited and proud rejection of Lady Lyle-Hackett's invitation, but the need to replenish a near empty poke won out.

'That seems fair, ma'am.' For a hundred dollars a man would work long and hard nursing cows or steering a plough, and end up with muscles that would take weeks to untangle, or a creaking butt.

'Shall we?' Lady Lyle-Hackett looped her arm through Strother's.

'Don't mind if I do, ma'am,' Strother replied.

As they strode along the boardwalk to the hotel, with Bambridge keeping a discreet distance, Strother began to wonder if his watch over Lady Lyle-Hackett would be an all-night vigil? If that were so, then it would explain that hundred dollars. He had heard of women who paid men to dally with them, but it had never made any sense at all to him. And it made even less sense when the woman smelled good, talked nice, was an aristo-whatever, and did not look like the rear end of a longhorn.

'Isn't that a wonderful moon,' she said.

'Yes, ma'am,' Strother agreed. 'That there is a Texas moon.'

'A Texas moon?' She laughed, and Strother heard the music of a thousand harps. 'But we're in Arizona,' she said with a twinkle in her eye that must have raised a lot of men's blood pressure.

'That's Texans for ya. They just can't stay in their own back yard,' Strother quipped.

Lady Lyle-Hackett's laughter deepened, and Strother had the kind of funny feeling he had had when he had gone out with Mary Kate Clark, a girl from a neighbouring farm, his first girl. And he was sure that this time there would be no talk about the price of hogs or the number of eggs laid by the Lyle-Hackett chickens.

'My name is Cecily,' she said. 'You call me that. I wouldn't want you to get arthritis of the jaw saying Lady Lyle-Hackett all the time.'

'Never reckoned on doing that, ma'am.'

'Your impudence will one day get you in trouble.'

'That, it's already done.'

'And what do I call you?'

'Jack will do just dandy.'

'Jack what?'

'Strother, ma'am.'

They strolled on to the hotel, untroubled. Strother would like to think that it was his presence that dissuaded any would-be bushwhackers. But in honesty, he had to admit that it was probably bowler-hat bringing up the rear who was having that effect. Recalling the manservant's trick with his head attire back in the saloon, were he to have any ideas of robbing the English rose on his arm, Jack Strother reckoned that he too would suppress any such urges.

On seeing Strother with Lady Cecily Lyle-Hackett on his arm, the hotel clerk who had earlier done everything he could to prevent Strother being a guest of the Diamond Place Hotel, now, after he got his jaw off his chest and his eyes back in their sockets, fawned over him.

'Will you be wanting supper, sir? A bath, sir? Would you like me to rustle up the town barber, Mr Strother?' This, on glancing at Lady Lyle-Hackett's creamy complexion, and the devastating effect Strother's week-old stubble would have on it.

'No need for any barber, clerk,' Cecily Lyle-Hackett purred, trickling her long and exquisitely moulded fingers along Strother's jaw. 'I think Jack's piratical look is quite fetching.'

'It surely is, Lady Lyle-Hackett, ma'am,' the clerk enthused.

Jack Strother chuckled. 'I didn't know you cared, mister.'

Flustered, the desk clerk began a long line of stammering that made no sense, because what got started never got finished.

'You are a card, aren't you, Jack,' Cecily chided Strother. 'Now you've embarrassed poor Mr Jones.'

As they headed upstairs, Jones called after them.

'I'll await your summons in the morning, Lady Lyle-Hackett,' he suggested, diplomatically.

On reaching what had been grandiosely named the presidential suite, following a ludicrous rumour that the

28

president would be stopping over when electioneering the previous year, Jack Strother's heartbeat quickened on the possibility of sharing Cecily Lyle-Hackett's bed. However, on a sudden flush of pride, foolish though it might be, Strother pulled back.

'Sorry, Cecily,' he apologized, with the vigour of a preacher denouncing sinful ways, 'but I'm a man who likes to choose, rather than be chosen. If you get my drift?'

Cecily Lyle-Hackett's laughter gave Strother the kind of sinking feeling that a man who's made a mule's rear end of himself gets.

'Bedding you was not my plan, Jack,' she said, her laughter getting even keener. 'You see, Bambridge sleeps with me.' Strother watched in gaping astonishment as the manservant entered the room. When he was out of earshot, she explained: 'Not in the same bed, of course.'

'But in the same room,' Strother said. 'Ain't that kind of . . . '

'Dangerous?'

'Yeah. I guess.'

'Not at all. You see, while serving in India in my father's regiment, Bambridge had an unfortunate experience at the hands of some villains that, as a conquestorial male, rendered him quite harmless.'

'Conquewhat?'

She leaned close to whisper in Strother's ear. He thought for a moment about what she had told him.

'Well,' he said, 'after that, he'd sure fit a saddle better.'

'Goodnight, Jack.'

After the room door closed, Strother remained in deep thought for a moment, shuddering at Lady Lyle-Hackett's revelation about what had happened to the unfortunate Bambridge. Then he headed for his own shoebox-sized room, which smelled of the last one hundred occupants, giving thanks that he had never visited India.

Preoccupied as he was with thoughts of Bambridge's misfortune and his own

very evident and very frustrated man-
hood, Strother walked into the room in
a fashion that was both stupid and very
unwise. A dark shadow leaped at him,
and he felt a searing pain in his left
arm, the arm he had instinctively raised
to defend himself. Though the pain of
the knife slash was terrible, it was the
lesser of two evils. Had he not raised
his arm, the blade would have slit his
throat open. He had foolishly forgotten
about Ben Bradley's spiteful sidekick,
Joe.

The slashing knife arced towards him
again.

3

Strother ducked under Joe's wild and desperate lunge and came up, fists balled, to crunch his attacker's groin. Joe let out an agonized howl and fell back nursing his genitals, his face contorted, the veins on his throat bulging to breaking point. Unmoved by his plight, Jack Strother swung a fist that he brought up from the floor. When it collided with the side of Joe's head, the ambusher's eyes almost popped clear from their sockets. He reeled across the room, tossed like a blade of straw in a twister, moaning as if a dozen devils were dragging him to hell. Still unmoved, Strother followed through with a series of quickly delivered punishing jabs that increased the pace of Joe's puppet-like dance until, with a final blow, he crashed through the window on to the roof of the hotel veranda. Joe's dead-weight proved too much for the structure. It groaned. One support beam bent and split, and three more quickly followed. By the time the sixth in the line snapped, the veranda had long since been doomed. The structure collapsed on to the street, a tumble of debris. Joe, oblivious to all that had happened from the instant he crashed through the window of Jack Strother's room, lay among the debris, out cold.

'Damn!' Strother swore, leaning out of the shattered window. 'Now I'm going to have to get me another room.'

So fierce had the tangle been that a crowd was piling out of the saloon. Along the street, Cranton, resisting the urge to satisfy his curiosity quickly, was coming from his office with the caution that long experience had taught him. Look long before leaping in.

Bringing up the tail-end of the saloon crowd was Ben Bradley. His flashing, malevolent look at Strother told him that his troubles were probably only beginning.

'Joe looks dead to me, Ben,' a scrawny specimen whom Strother had seen sucking up to Bradley earlier in the saloon, opined.

'Well, go and check, you noggin' head!' Bradley yelled at the man.

The man did as he was instructed and reported back a moment later.

'Got a pulse. But it's real jittery, Ben.'

'Then get him to Doc Brandy!'

Three men stepped forward on the click of Bradley's fingers to carry Joe to the sawbone's office further along the street.

The incensed Bradley turned his glaring eyes on the marshal who, now that he had not seen any immediate danger to his hide, was arriving at a run. Bradley nodded in Strother's direction.

'Do your job, Cranton,' he ordered.

'Sure, Ben,' the lawman readily agreed, dispensing with any attempt at getting an explanation of events.

'He tried to slit my throat,' Strother called down to the street. 'But I guess that doesn't matter any,' he added, resigned to having his side of the story unheard.

'You're going to jail for grievious assault, if not outright murder, mister,' Cranton said.

'I figure we shouldn't bother with jail, Marshal,' Ben Bradley snarled.

The lawman shifted uneasy feet, trying to avoid the hole opening up under him.

'I'm not sure that I know what you mean, Ben,' he muttered.

'Sure you do, Cranton!' Bradley barked.

'W-well, Ben,' the lackey marshal stammered, mindful of a fellow lawman who had allowed a lynching and was now breaking rocks, 'an illegal hanging might bring a US marshal to these parts.'

'We'll think about that if and when it happens.'

Listening to the exchanges, and aware of the dangers, Jack Strother reckoned that it was time to make a point. He fetched the rifle he had left standing against the wall behind the room door and hurried back to the window, just as Cranton was crumbling.

'I guess you're right at that, Ben. And I figure that this man is a danger and a menace to this whole town, don't you?'

'Yeah! Yeah!' was Bradley's impatient response. 'I figure that no one's safe in their beds with a mad dog like Strother on the loose. And you know what happens to mad dogs, don't you, Marshal?'

Cranton settled his gunbelt on his beefy hips.

'Sure I do, Ben.'

When the marshal turned and walked towards the hotel, his steps were brought up short by the spitting bullets kissing the toecaps of his boots from Strother's Winchester. The crowd that had piled out of the saloon scurried back inside, with Ben Bradley leading the charge.

Marshal Sam Cranton looked behind him for support and found that he was totally alone.

'Marshal,' Jack Strother intoned, 'I reckon that you should give the matter of my demise some thought. Like I said, all I gave that *hombre* was what he deserved, nothing more and nothing less.'

'W-w-well,' Cranton's stammer was like the spit of a Gatling-gun. He glanced behind him again in the hope that support might have materialized. It had not, and Cranton shuddered in his boots. 'Maybe we could talk about this?' was his meek suggestion.

'Cranton! Don't you even think about backing off,' Ben Bradley roared from the saloon.

'But, B-Ben . . . '

Sixgun bullets bit the ground behind him.

'Looks like you've got yourself in a real bind, Marshal,' Strother drawled.

'Caught as you are between two ornery critters. And all you've got to do, is make up your mind as to which is the ornerier, friend.'

'Flush him out, Cranton,' Bradley commanded.

'Sure, Ben.'

The marshal's bravado lasted all of a second before Jack Strother's steely warning had him swinging back towards him, as dithery as a bride on her wedding night.

'I don't aim to go quietly to a hangman's rope, Marshal.'

The stand-off dragged on, becoming more tense by the second, until a window further along the hotel was raised and Lady Lyle-Hackett poked her head out.

'Would someone shoot someone and get all this nonsense over with, or else go back to bed. A girl needs her sleep, gentlemen.'

'Her ladyship's got a point, I reckon,' Strother opined.

'Mebbe we could settle this come

morning, Ben?' was the marshal's hopeful suggestion.

'That would be much more civilized, Mr Bradley . . . Ben,' Cecily Lyle-Hackett cajoled, in a husky voice that Jack Strother figured would bring to life a dead man's lady-pleaser. And he was far from dead.

'Darling,' she added for good measure, in the kind of throaty way that would have a coyote howling all night long.

Ben Bradley melted like a snowball on a hot gridle. 'If that's your wish, Cecily,' he said, with more purr in his voice that a well-fed cat, his mind obviously running ahead to another meeting with the English aristocrat.

'Then I'll say goodnight, gentlemen,' she said, slamming the window shut.

'See you fellas in my office in the morning?' Cranton said.

'I'll be there,' Strother said.

'Me, too,' Bradley added. 'But I ain't going to forget how yella you were tonight, Cranton.'

'Me, yella, Ben?' the lawman crooned.

'As a darn daisy!' Bradley growled.

Cranton backed off, and hurried away to the law office and its privy outback, hoping that he would not be too late.

The scrawny man who had been one of the trio who had carried Joe to the doc's office came back out to report that he would survive.

'Who gives a shit!' Ben Bradley railed. 'Go tell him that tomorrow he can collect his pay and clear out.'

'Nice feller,' Strother mumbled, pulling his head back from the shattered window. He was of a mind to seek a change of room but, the night being balmy, he reckoned that he would not die of the cold. Exhausted, he fell on to the bed and was instantly asleep. He did not fear an attack by Bradley. Smitten, as Strother suspected he was, he'd not be eager to displease her ladyship.

★　★　★

When Strother went downstairs the next morning, the clerk informed him that breakfast, which did not come with his room, had been arranged for by Lady Lyle-Hackett. Strother went through to the fancy dining-room where, in his trail clothes, he looked as out of place as a saint in a whore house.

Noses turned up as he went past, and a couple of delicate ladies paled as his combination of horse and trail wafted their way. It wasn't that he was dirty, he had washed the previous night at the town pump, but after a long spell on the trail it took a time to wash away the peculiar scent of living, eating and sleeping with your nag on ground that had soaked up blood, sweat and manure. In a short while he had the dining-room to himself. Breakfast tucked away, he headed for the law office.

On entering the marshal's office, he came up short on seeing Lady Lyle-Hackett cuddling up to Ben Bradley.

'Ben,' she cooed, 'let there be no more of this silliness between you and

Mr Strother.' She nibbled his ear, and purred, 'Darling.'

'Sure, Cecily, honey,' Bradley eagerly agreed. 'If Strother is willing.'

Sam Cranton flashed anxious and pleading eyes Strother's way.

'Oh, I'm sure Mr Strother won't be difficult. Will you Mr Strother?'

'No, ma'am.' He turned and walked out. Waiting outside on guard duty was Bambridge, her ladyship's bowler-hatted protector, looking distressed.

'You don't look so good, Bambridge', was Strother's comment.

'It's her ladyship's rather unsuitable assignation with Mr Bradley that troubles me,' the manservant confided. He leaned closer to unburden himself further. 'You see, Mr Strother, her ladyship is looking for a husband — '

'Ben Bradley?' Strother scoffed. 'A suitable husband for an English aristocrat?'

'When I say suitable, sir,' Bambridge explained patiently, 'of course, I mean in a purely monetary sense.'

'In a what sense?'

Bambridge smiled, if that's what a shark's grin could be described as.

'Money, dear sir. Lots of it. You see, Lady Lyle-Hackett finds herself in financial straits.'

'Yeah,' Strother snorted. 'She's staying in the swankiest suite in the hotel. Dresses in the finest clothes. Eats grub fit for a king. Heck, I'd like to be so straited, fella.'

'It's called keeping up appearances, Mr Strother,' Bambridge educated him. 'But I assure you, m'lady's finacial situation is most precarious.'

'So, you're telling me that she wants to suck Bradley dry?'

Bambridge grimaced. 'In a purely financial sense, Mr Strother.'

'What if I walked in there and told him?'

'Believe me, Mr Strother, you'd never make it,' said Bambridge in a voice barely above a whisper. Jack Strother believed him. Then, good naturedly, Bambridge added: 'But I'm sure that you would not wish to harm or offend her ladyship in any way. Good day, sir.'

'And good day to you,' Strother flung back as he walked away.

Anxious to shake off the dust of Bradley Creek, he decided to postpone replenishing his supplies until he reached Willsburg, and headed for the livery. His business in the troublesome burg was over, and it was time to hit the trail.

He was about three miles out of town when a fast-clipping rider caught him up.

4

'You're wanted back in town, pronto,' the young messenger told Strother.

'I am,' was Strother's amazed response, flicking back the black fringe of hair from his forehead. 'What for?'

His immediate thoughts were that some hitch relative to the events of the night before had arisen. Like, maybe, Joe had taken on wings. But if that were the case, it would have been a posse on his tail instead of a youngster barely out of breeches. Or maybe, Strother liked to think, Lady Lyle-Hackett had found that, gone, she missed him.

'Doc Brandy sent me,' the boy informed Strother. 'Says it's awful urgent. This old-timer he's got dyin' wants to jaw with ya.' To clarify further, the messenger elaborated. 'The old-timer you stood up to Ben Bradley for yesterday.'

'Why would he want to talk to me?' was Strother's puzzled answer.

'Dunno. But Doc says to tell ya that he ain't got much wind left in him, and that you'd better hurry.'

Jack Strother looked to the trail ahead. 'Going back . . . ? I don't know, son. Can't be anything that urgent. I don't even know the old man.'

The youngster looked shocked.

'It ain't right not to listen to a man's dyin' words, mister,' he said, critically.

After a moment's further deliberation, Strother agreed.

'Guess it ain't at that, young feller.'

The young messenger swung his horse.

'I know a fast trail back to town.'

'Lead the way, then.'

During the relatively short and pacy ride back to town, Strother racked his brains for the reason why the old-timer would want to talk to him, and was as wise on reaching Bradley Creek as he had been on setting out on the return journey.

'What the hell are you doing back in

town?' Ben Bradley demanded to know when he saw him hitching his horse to the rail outside the town infirmary. He shifted his stance. 'You ain't fixing on more trouble, are you? 'Cause if you are . . . '

Bradley let the threat hang in the air.

'He's here to see that old-timer he stood up agin you for yesterday, Mr Bradley,' the youngster said. 'He's sucking his last air.'

'What would the old man have to say to you?' Bradley questioned Strother with belligerent curiosity.

'Can't say,' Strother replied. 'But whatever it is, it surely's none of your goddam business, Bradley.'

Bradley was about to react, but his mind was changed by Lady Lyle-Hackett's appearance from the milliner's shop, sporting a hat that Strother reckoned would be more attractive to a vulture for nesting in than a head for wearing it on. But when it turned out that the hat was a present from Ben Bradley, its wearing became clear. To get her hands on the Bradley fortune, Jack Strother reckoned that Cecily Lyle-Hackett would wear a crown of cow-dung.

'My, you look a picture, Cecily,' Bradley enthused. 'I'll get us a rig and we'll ride out to the ranch right now.'

'Your name Strother?'

Strother swung around to answer the man's summons. The tailcoat and side-whiskers marked him as a professional man — the town doctor, Strother guessed.

'Yep.'

'Then if you want to hear what the old-timer's got to say, you'd better get yourself inside fast.'

The old-timer's eyes opened and rolled when the doc shook him, none too gently in Strother's opinion; an opinion he voiced.

'Shaking doesn't matter now,' Doc Brandy replied brusquely, and left.

The old-timer gripped Jack Strother's hand and pulled him close. When he spoke, his voice was like the scrape of a nail.

'In my right trousers' pocket.'

Strother searched the old man's pocket and came up with a rawhide pouch.

'Open it.'

Strother opened the pouch and saw something glisten in its dark interior.

'Take it out,' the old-timer said impatiently. 'I ain't got much time left.'

Strother rolled the huge diamond in the palm of his hand.

'It's gen'ine,' the old-timer assured him. 'Got it from an old 'Pache. Found him dying in the desert. Nursed him until he died. Said that there's a whole cave full of gold and diamonds where that one came from.'

Brandy, curious, had left the infirmary door ajar as he departed to facilitate his eavesdropping. His heart staggered dangerously as his eyes lit on the diamond. And on hearing the old man's tale, his heart raced even faster still.

The old-timer paused to draw a croaking breath.

'Ain't no good to me now. This 'Pache called it Raoul's Treasure. Ever heard of a critter called Raoul?'

Strother shook his head.

' 'Pache said that this Raoul's Treasure is in a place called Devil's Canyon. Ever heard of that?'

Strother shook his head again.

'Me neither.'

'Didn't you ask the Indian?'

'Died before I got round to it.' The old-timer grinned. 'If he did, Jethro and me would have long ago shook the dust of the West off, and be living like kings in one of them big cities back East.'

'Jethro?'

The old-timer grabbed his chest. His face contorted with pain, and his eyes bulged.

'Damn heart o' mine,' he complained. His grip on Strother tightened. 'Thank ya kindly for taking a stand yesterday against that cur Ben Bradley.' The old man's back arched and a great gush of air escaped his lips. His eyes spun and closed. His body sagged, and seemed only half the size it had been a second before.

'Doc!' Strother hailed.

Brandy delayed his entrance to the infirmary, not wanting to raise any suspicion by seeming too close at hand. He had heard many dying men's tales, yarns in their heads which they believed to be true, but somehow the old man's story had the ring of truth to it.

'Hurry,' Strother urged.

'No point in rushing. The old man's heart was on a string. Say what he had to say?'

'He said it,' Strother confirmed.

'You burying him?'

'Burying him?' Strother yelped. 'I ain't got the poke.'

'Then I guess he'll have to go in the community hole. With the town having to cough up, he'll not get anything more than the back of a mule and a shovel of earth.'

Jack Strother looked at the diamond cupped in the palm of his hand.

'Said it was a diamond.'

Nathan Brandy scoffed dismissively. 'You believe him?'

'I'm not sure. But why would a dying man want to lie?'

'He probably wasn't — lying, I mean. A man goes funny in the head near dying. I mean if that was a genuine diamond, it would be worth a fortune. And why would any man with a fortune die penniless?'

Strother looked again at the diamond and saw the way it reflected the sunshine streaming through the infirmary window, a sparkling kaleidescope of light.

'Ever see a diamond before?' Brandy asked.

Jack Strother shook his head. No, he had never seen a diamond before, but he had heard that they sparkled just like what he was holding in his hand.

'I did,' the sawbones said, and stated postively, 'and that is not a diamond.' When Strother was not fully convinced, he added, 'Where would a grubby old-timer get his hands on a diamond that size, in fact any diamond at all, big or small?'

'He had an explanation for that.'

'Oh? What explanation would that be?' Brandy asked, but already knew.

Jack Strother was about to relate the old man's tale about the old Apache whom the old-timer had helped and comforted. How he had given him the diamond in return for his kindness. And how there was a whole treasure belonging to some fella called Raoul in a place called Devil's Canyon. But recalling the way the sawbones had left the infimary door partly open when he left, he reckoned that him telling the old-timer's story would be old news.

'Heck,' Strother sighed. 'I guess you're right, the old-timer got dead man's loco, Doc.' He rolled the diamond in the palm of his hand, for he was now convinced that that was what it was. 'I guess this is just a trinket.'

He turned to leave.

'It's a nice piece of fancy glass. I'll give you a couple of dollars for it, if you want,' Nathan Brandy casually offered.

Strother turned back.

'Yeah,' he said enthusiastically. Then, frowning: 'I need more than a couple of dollars to plant the old-timer.'

The doc looked with disdain at the corpse.

'Don't worry about him. Doesn't much matter to a man like that how he's buried.'

'Maybe not,' Strother said, his tone hard. 'But it matters a hell of a lot to me.' He turned to leave again.

'Ten dollars.'

Again Strother turned back.

'For a piece of fancy glass?'

Brandy shrugged and grinned.

'I'm a fool. You see, this lady I know . . . Well, I figure she'd like it.'

Strother made a pretence of considering Brandy's offer, but his mind was already made up.

'No, Doc. I reckon I'll sell my horse to cover the cost of the old-timer's funeral.' He rolled the diamond in the palm of his hand, brilliant light showering from it. 'Ain't never got a present before, you see, even if it's only glass.' His face became a mask of marvel. 'Will you just look at how the light shines from this fancy glass. Be seeing you, Doc.' Walking to the infirmary door, he could feel the burn of the sawbones' eyes on his back.

'Selling your horse would leave you stranded,' he said. Strother did not break his stride. 'OK. I'll bury the old man and give you . . . oh, say, twenty dollars.'

Strother paused. 'Mighty generous,' was his opinion. 'You must really like this woman.'

Nathan Brandy chuckled in a man-to-man fashion.

'She's a lot younger. I need an edge.'

'Makes sense.'

'Do we have a deal?'

Strother's casualness belied his unease. He had seen men go haywire before, given the chance to get their hands on riches, and the doc had that look; the look of money-fever that would gnaw away at him until nothing else but getting his hands on the diamond would matter.

Strother had a dilemma. He wanted the old-timer to have a decent burial, which he could not pay for. And as the sawbones said, without a horse he'd be trapped in Bradley Creek, the object of a lot of curiosity and in a whole pile of danger.

Of course he could try and sell the diamond, but who in Bradley Creek could afford to purchase it for anything remotely near its true value. He would have to part with it for a fraction of its worth. His plan would be to take the diamond back East where its true value could be assessed and a deal struck. He should clear out of town right away, but he'd have sleepless nights knowing that the old-timer was buried in a pauper's grave, when he had been so generous to him. It surely was a giant-sized headache. He needed time to think.

'I'll chew on your offer, Doc' he said. 'But I reckon we'll have a deal.'

When Strother left, Brandy staggered, so drained was he by the tension when it looked as though he would not strike a deal. And now, with the excitement of having done so, he was going to be a very rich man — very rich indeed. He dreamed of travel to far-flung places, where there were paved streets and where there would be no clinging dust that got into a man's pores and clogged his gullet. And where the air would not be pungent with the stench of animals and unwashed people. He'd see the great operas performed. Go to London and see the swank theatres and the posh gentlemen's clubs he'd read about. And he'd never have to inhale another foul breath, or lance a pus-filled boil. And most of all, he'd be free of his wife Hetty. Ugly and whingeing Hetty.

Then, inveitably, greed fuelled greed. What if he could get his hands on this Raoul's Treasure which the old man spoke of? He'd be as rich as a king; richer than he could even dream of being. His breath caught painfully in his lungs. He felt faint at the very thought. His mind's eyes imagined a glistening treasure-trove.

Sensing a presence behind him, Nathan Brandy swung around, and his eyes popped wide.

5

'Howdy.' A man the dead spit of the old-timer who had just died, greeted Brandy. So alike was he, that the sawbones quickly checked that the dead man was in fact still dead.

On hearing Brandy's screech, Jack Strother doubled back into the infirmary, and came up short on seeing the look-alike old-timer.

'My brother Ike,' he explained to Strother, pointing to the dead man. 'Twins, we was.'

Mystery solved. 'You're Jethro?' Strother asked.

'That's me.' He looked with a deep sadness at Ike. 'I'll miss the ornery old critter.' Then his sadness turned to a dry chuckle. 'We had many a good time fooling folk. Or,' he looked at the pallor-stricken doctor, 'scaring folk, too.' His mournfulness returned. 'Wish

I'd stayed in town with Ike, and hadn't gone back to dally with a widow-woman back along the trail. I'd have been around to hear Ike's last words. I'm sure as hell he had some, 'cause he was a real mouthy kinda fella, was Ike Billings.'

Regretfully, Jack Strother took the rawhide pouch containing the diamond from his pocket and handed it over to Jethro.

'This is rightly yours, I reckon.'

Jethro Billings looked at the glistening stone in his palm.

'Is it real?' Strother asked.

'Wouldn't know. Ike prob'ly thought it was.' Jethro Billings studied Strother. 'He must have respected you a great deal, mister. I heard what happened in town yesterday. Your stand against Bradley would have made a real big impression on Ike, I guess.' He handed back the diamond. 'You keep it, it's yours.'

Strother protested, 'You're kin, Jethro.'

'If it's what Ike wanted, that's the way it's got to be.'

'If you'd been here when he was dying — '

'He'd still give you the diamond.' He looked at his dead twin. 'Though we was twins, Ike was diff'rent from me. Honourable and arrow-straight to a fault. Never approved of my womanizing and drinking.' He gently brushed back Ike's sparse grey hair from his high, sun-burnished forehead. 'If I didn't do as he wanted in life, then I'm damn well going to do it now.'

He turned to Strother.

'The diamond is yours, mister!' He shoved the stone back into Strother's hand. 'Got a monicker?'

'Jack Strother.'

'Pleased to meet you, Jack Strother.'

Strother shook the old man's gnarled right hand.

'Ike had this story about a treasure — Raoul's Treasure.'

Jethro Billings shrugged.

'Don't know nothing 'bout no treasure, Jack.'

'He said an old Apache he came

across in the desert who was dying told him about the treasure. Said it was in a place called Devil's Canyon.'

'I stayed behind in Mexico. Ike came on ahead. We were to meet up here, only I got here first and then went back aways along the trail to that widow-woman. But not before I crossed paths with Ben Bradley and his sidekick.'

Strother now understood Joe's confusion of the day before in thinking he had ordered Ike Billings out of town. It was in fact Jethro he had tangled with.

Jethro sighed contentedly.

'Rosita Gonzalez was quite a woman.' His cloudy blue eyes lit up with mischief. 'Widow-woman wasn't bad either.'

'Do you know where this Devil's Canyon is?' Strother enquired.

Jethro frowned.

'The country where Ike would have crossed paths with the 'Pache's got a whole heap of canyons, most without names. And those that have names, have different names to the 'Pache and the white man.'

62

'So when the Indian said Devil's Canyon, it might be known by another name, too?'

'Even a coupla other names.' Jethro became thoughtful. 'There's a canyon I know of that puts the wind up Indians. Don't know it's name. But it's got these three boulders in it that look like they're watching folk, in case they get up to any mischief. The Indians was real scared of those stones. Possessed by evil spirits, they figured. Bad med'cine, the 'Pache reckoned. Wouldn't go next or near that canyon, 'Paches.'

Jack Strother was excited.

'You could find this canyon?' he quizzed.

Jethro scratched at the stubble on his chin.

'Mebbe,' was his wary conclusion. 'One canyon looks pretty much like t'other in those parts. But . . . ' His brief flourish of excitement turned to stark doubt. 'I guess Ike must have looked good and proper,' his gaze went to his poorly clad, trail dusty twin, 'and found nothing.'

'I guess,' Strother said, his hope on a downward spiral.

'Unless Ike came on here first to hook up with me afore we both went looking.'

So preoccupied by their intense speculation were Strother and Billings that they had ignored Nathan Brandy. To both men, a professional man like the doctor would have no interest in their jabbering, having no need to dream silly dreams about treasure, unlike a man whose only possessions were his horse and the clothes he stood up in. But had they taken the time to look, they would have seen a strange metamorphosis taking hold of the sawbones. The kind of incurable fever that they would have recognized as the brain-twisting sickness that infected men who dreamed of riches. It was the kind of sickness that took hold of men in a gold rush.

'Figure you and me should try and find this Raoul's Treasure, Jack?' Jethro asked. He stuck out a tongue that was as dry as desert sand. 'Mebbe we could talk it over in the saloon,' he suggested. His cloudy blue eyes became dreamy. 'Imagine, Jack, a whole pile of diamonds and gold.'

'I'm imagining, Jethro.' Strother sighed, Billings's dreaminess was proving infectious.

'We could live like kings, Jack.'

'Yeah.' Then Strother came back to earth with a crash. 'Eyewash!'

'Huh?'

'You heard me. It's all eyewash. Raoul's Treasure, my ass.'

'Why would the 'Pache lie, Jack? He was dying.'

'Maybe he was loco.'

'Mebbe he was. But what if he wasn't?'

For a lengthy spell Jack Strother weighed up Billings's reasoning.

'Sure,' he muttered. 'What if he wasn't?'

★ ★ ★

On leaving Doc Brandy's office, Strother collided with Cecily Lyle-Hackett, and the diamond he still held in his hand clattered to the boardwalk. He instantly retrieved it, but knew as her eyes latched on to the stone that it was genuine and that she coveted the jewel.

'Hello, Jack,' she greeted in a honeyed tone.

'You coming or not?' Ben Bradley called from the rig he was seated in, his displeasure at Cecily Lyle-Hackett's dalliance with Strother raising his hackles. The English beauty looked with haughty annoyance at the rancher who, unwisely, delivered an ultimatum.

'I'm making tracks right now.'

'Then don't let me delay you, Mr Bradley,' she replied dismissively.

'You mean you ain't coming?' Bradley barked, astounded.

'That's exactly what I mean,' Cecily confirmed. She looped her arm through Strother's. 'I'm remaining in town with Jack.'

Ben Bradley had enough anger in him to blow smoke out of his ears.

'I should have killed you when I had the chance, Strother,' he growled. He abandoned the rig and vaulted on to his horse. 'The next time we cross paths, I will!'

When Bradley's dust cleared, Lady Lyle-Hackett guided Strother towards the hotel.

'I think we've got a lot to talk about, Jack,' she purred.

Gently but firmly, he disengaged from her.

'Don't reckon we have, ma'am. I've already got a partner.' He turned to Billings. 'Jethro, I figure we should hit the trail, don't you?'

'I'm ready, Jack,' Billings enthused.

Enraged, Cecily Lyle-Hackett watched Jack Strother walk away. Rejection was something entirely new to her. Up to now she had found men easy to manipulate. Strother was the first man who had had the gumption to turn tail on her, and that excited her as a woman. What also excited her even more was the fortune Strother had held in the palm of his hand. She knew a genuine diamond when she saw one. And the one she had just seen would put the Lyle-Hacketts back on the English aristocratic map.

'Let's go find that Raoul fella's treasure.'

At that moment, Jack Strother would have gladly throttled the old-timer. Cecily Lyle-Hackett had almost smothered her excitement on hearing Jethro's pronouncement, but not quite. Could the Raoul the old man had spoken of possibly be Hernando Raoul? she wondered, her heart skittering at the very possibility. Raoul had been a Spanish adventurer who scoured the South Americas for treasure, and didn't much care how he got his hands on it, amassing an Aladdin's cave from his ruthless plundering.

As a child back in England, she had heard the story of Raoul's Treasure from a Spanish guest at Hackett Hall and had thought it a terrific yarn, but nothing more. But what if Señor Valdez's tale had a lot more substance to it than she had thought back then.

'The last that was heard of Raoul was when he became ill near the Mexican border,' their Spanish guest had told his hosts. 'It was said that he made good use of his skills as an engineer, which had been his profession before he became an adventurer, to hide his bounty, using the small army of African slaves who were with him to do his bidding.

Hernando Raoul was a very clever man. On a trip to New Orleans, he learned some magic tricks from a French circus magician, and used these simple tricks to hold the ignorant and fearful slaves in awe and fear of him, telling them that he could steal their souls if they disobeyed him. The magician's tricks were enough to convince the superstitious slaves that he had godlike powers.'

'Has the treasure been found, Señor

Valdez?' Cecily had asked excitedly.

'No, my little one,' had been his answer.

'Then these slaves must know where Raoul's Treasure can be found?' she said breathlessly, her imagination fired by thoughts of the massive wealth to be claimed if the story were not a fairy-tale. 'Find them, and they will lead us to the treasure. It's all so simple, *señor*.'

Even then, though only a child, she was becoming aware of her father's precarious financial state, evidenced by the reduced number of servants and the fall-off in dinner and week-end guests. An incurable gambler and a stupid businessman, Rupert Lyle-Hackett had squandered the family fortune on slow horses, bad cards and silly ventures, including a string of illicit affairs with women who found it as easy to part him from his money as it was for them to part with their virtue.

Valdez had laughed and playfully

twigged her nose, much to her annoyance. At thirteen Cecily Lyle-Hackett considered herself to be past that kind of silly adult behaviour.

'Señor Raoul was a greedy man. Even though he was dying himself and his treasure was useless to him, he did not want anyone else to have it. Raoul had learned another skill, that of potion witchery. When the elaborate work was finished on his treasure cave, he prepared a poisonous brew and fed it to the slaves. All died except one, the man who told the story of Raoul's Treasure, shortly before he was hanged for stealing a loaf of bread from his master's kitchen.

'So you see my young one, Raoul's Treasure will never be found.'

'Someone must know where it is,' she had said desperately.

'Perhaps some Indians, who the slave mentioned had been watching them. It is said that he gave the Apache Indians a fabulous diamond whose sparkling light frightened them. Raoul told them that a powerful god lived inside the diamond, who would wreak revenge on them if they harmed him. Allied to the frightened behaviour of the African slaves, it was easy to convince the Apaches that to harm him would in turn bring harm to themselves. A very shrewd man, Señor Raoul.'

Cecily had leaped off her chair.

'Then someone does know where the treasure is!'

Señor Valdez had laughed. Being one of Spain's wealthiest noblemen, it was easy for him to take the story of Raoul's Treasure so lightly; he did not suffer the nightmares she had about ending up in the work-house.

'Maybe the treasure is nothing more than an interesting and amusing party tale, my little one.'

For a time after Señor Valdez had told the story of Raoul's Treasure, Cecily Lyle-Hackett had dreamed of finding it and restoring the family's dwindling fortunes. But soon after, the harsh consequences of her father's idiocy came home to roost, when his creditors forced him to sell Hackett Hall and most of the estate to settle his mounting debts, and the family had been forced to live in what had previously been the gate lodge by the patronage and generosity of the new owner of the estate. Leisurely, carefree days, were replaced by worry and sleepless nights. The family's struggle for survival left no room for day-dreaming. And in the fight to survive, she had forgotten about Luis Valdez's tale of Raoul's Treasure.

Her brother, unable to live with shame and loss of privilege, had hanged himself. Her mother, whom Cecily blamed and despised for closing her eyes and mind to the plight which her father's silly excesses had pitched them into, simply faded away like an autumn leaf. Defeated and bemused, her father had wandered off one day and disappeared, until he was found dead in London in the company of street ruffians a year later, apparently training to become a pickpocket. She had generously been taken in by family friends who had treated her with kindness, and in a custom befitting her birth. During this respite from the drudgery of trying to survive, she began to hope again of one day finding Raoul's Treasure and reclaiming Hackett Hall. Rupert Lyle-Hackett had not had much time for *mere girls*. But were it to happen that it was she who restored the fortune and pride of the Lyle-Hacketts, she would mock him for the remainder of her life, and for eternity beyond her mortal existence.

Señor Valdez had leaned more towards the opinion that the tale of Raoul's Treasure had more myth than substance, and this too, after her initial fervour, had become Cecily's belief. But now she could feel the fire of her childhood excitement inside her. What if the diamond which Jack Strother possessed was the diamond Hernando Raoul had given to the Apache Indians? Just a tiny part of the fabulous treasure he had plundered. The thought threatened to stop her heart.

'A dangerous woman,' was Jethro Billings's opinion, as he walked with Jack Strother to the general store to purchase the supplies they needed.

Strother nodded in agreement.

'But what a woman, Jethro,' he said with a wry grin.

The old-timer scratched his stubbled chin and smirked slyly.

'Yeah, Jack. What a woman, indeed.'

Watching them from the infirmary window, Nathan Brandy's eyes were panic-stricken on seeing where, he reckoned, Strother and the old-timer were heading. The general store for supplies! Once Strother and the old-timer rode out, his chance to get his hands on Raoul's Treasure would be gone.

He needed time to think and plan, therefore he had to prevent Strother and the old man from leaving town. With this intention, he hurried ahead and entered the general store through the rear.

'What the heck, Nathan!' Larry Saunders, the store-owner yelped when, looking up from his accounts, he found Brandy standing alongside him, as pale and drawn as a ghost.

'See those fellas coming this way.' The doctor pointed through the store window.

'The drifter and the old-timer?'

'Yes. They're coming to get supplies.'

'Good,' Saunders enthused. 'Business has been slow of late.'

'Only you're not going to let them have those supplies, Larry.'

The store-owner was puzzled and a touch resentful at having his business dictated to him.

'I ain't? Why not?' he asked.

'Because if they leave town, a fortune goes with them, Larry.'

The store-owner looked at the scruffy pair coming his way and shook his head.

'If you ask me, you should stay away from your own potions, Nathan.'

Brandy hated having to share his

knowledge of Raoul's Treasure with anyone, but if he did not, he would throw away any hope of getting his hands on the treasure.

'Close up, Larry,' he urged. 'Then I'll tell you all about Raoul's Treasure.'

The store-owner's interest perked up.

'Raoul's Treasure, you say?'

Nathan Brandy's eyes narrowed.

'You've heard of Raoul?'

'Yeah.'

'Where? From whom?'

'Looks like we've both got stories to tell, Nathan,' Saunders said, hurrying to put up the closed sign on the shop door. Scurrying back, he pulled the sawbones down behind the counter out of sight, just as Jack Strother and Jethro Billings tried the door.

'Makes no sense, a general store being closed at this time,' was Jethro's opinion.

'Surely doesn't, Jethro,' Strother agreed.

But though he had no evidence of such, he guessed that the reason for the store's closure was in some way related to their needing its services. When they had gone Saunders escorted the town doctor to a room at the rear of the store, where Nathan Brandy told his story.

'A diamond,' he shaped his fist, 'that size, Larry,' he finished.

Saunders shook his head in doubt. He shaped his fist.

'Ain't no diamond that size, Nathan.'

'Yes, there damn well is,' the doctor said, annoyed by Saunders' doubting his word. 'I've seen it with my own eyes.'

Finally convinced, Saunders' reaction was, 'I'll be damned!'

'And it's just a tiny part of the whole treasure,' Brandy enthused.

Breathless, the storekeeper quizzed Brandy.

'Raoul, you say this Spaniard's name was? I heard about this *hombre*. Coming out here on the wagon train, there was this fella from a place called Barcelona, that's in Spain — '

'I know where Barcelona is, Larry,' the sawbones said sharply.

'Well, this gent got skunk drunk one night when me and him were on watch. Rambled on about this fella Raoul. Said that he had come to America to find this Raoul's Treasure. I thought he was talking through his rear end, the way a fella does when he's all liquored up.'

'Looking, you say? Brandy fretted.

'Had this map an' all.'

'Map!' The sawbones groaned, seeing the vast riches he had been dreaming of slipping from his grasp.

'Don't get so peppered up, Nathan,' Saunders said, grabbing Brandy's arm to steady him. 'This *hombre* from Barcelona never got near finding Raoul's Treasure. Got caught by a fiery-headed Irishman with his hand up his wife's petticoats. Killed him there and then.'

Brandy's relief was immense, until another dreadful thought came to mind.

'This map you say the Spaniard had,

what happened to it?'

Saunders shrugged.

'The last I saw of it was when the Spaniard put it back in a tin box he kept it in. During the night Donegal Ned, the Irishman, killed him. Guess it was buried with him.'

'Buried with him?' Nathan Brandy felt faint. 'And you didn't try and get your hands on it?'

'Heck, Nathan. Like I said, this Spaniard was skunk drunk. I figured that this Raoul's Treasure came right out of the bottle he was supping from.'

'Well, I guess that's that,' Brandy said despondently.

'Ain't necessarily so.' Brandy's eyes darted Saunders' way, sparking with hope. 'If we find the Spaniard's grave, we find the tin box, I figure. It would take a long time for a tin box to decay. That map is probably still as good as new.'

'Did this gent from Barcelona ever mention a place called Devil's Canyon?'

Saunders shook his head.

'Have you ever heard of such a place?'

The storekeeper shook his head again.

'Never mind.'

The sawbones' next statement brought Saunders crashing back to reality.

'All we've got to do is get our hands on that map.'

Seeing the store-owner's shoulders slump, Nathan Brandy's heart took on a dangerously erratic beat. His gloom deepened.

'You could find his grave again, couldn't you, Larry?' he asked.

The storekeeper's shoulders drooped more.

'It was a long time ago, Nathan. All of ten years. And it was open country.'

'There must be some landmark you can recall,' Brandy pleaded in desperation. 'A canyon? A creek? A damn mountain?' he wailed, as Saunders kept shaking his head. After a moment's total despair, the sawbones brightened up with his next idea. 'How far from Bradley Creek were you when the Irishman killed the Spaniard, Larry?'

'A day, maybe a little more, as I recall. This was just a tent-town back then. Didn't want to stop here, but my wagon busted a wheel and the train moved on before I could get it repaired. The town blacksmith was drunk for four whole days. Waited for the next train to come through, but it was two years before it did, and by then I was — '

'Shut up, Larry,' Brandy interjected. 'Let me think. If we can find Raoul's Treasure, you'll not have to weigh a pound of butter or heft a sack of beans ever again. And I won't have to live with the stink of sickness.

'What we've got to do, is retrace your journey. Stands to reason that in a day or so, because that's the time it took the wagon train to reach this burg, we'll be right back to where that Spaniard is buried. Once there, I'm sure that something will jerk your mind, Larry.'

The storekeeper saw little if any merit in Brandy's plan.

'But while we're going back, those hobos will be heading for the treasure, Nathan,' he worried.

Dreaming of riches was dandy, but he had a *get by* living from the store, and the thought of throwing it away by going on a wild-goose chase and letting someone else grab his business had a sobering effect. He balanced that with the fact that, of late, he had thought about moving on. Bradley Creek had not grown as it had promised, and it was now unlikely to expand much beyond its present limits, if in fact it did not shrink. And though he was limber yet, there was no ignoring the pains in his joints and spine that in time would make the work of a storekeeper a painful grind.

Shrewdly sensing Saunders' mood, Brandy tempted him.

'All we've got to lose by trying is time, Larry. And maybe we won't have to come back to this one-horse town ever again.'

Saunders yielded to Brandy's temptation.

'Let's do it, Nathan,' he said.

6

Suspicious of the reason for the general store's closure, Jack Strother went to the rear of the store to investigate further. The store could have been closed for a perfectly good reason, of course, but he reckoned that its premature shut down was not innocent, and was intended to deny him and Jethro the supplies they needed. And the only reason he could see for the storekeeper's reluctance to do business with them was to delay their departure. He thought back to his and Jethro's loose talk in the infirmary. Strother ducked behind a stack of crates when he saw Nathan Brandy leave by the store's back door, his excitement evidently matched by the storekeeper's. And the reason for their elation was right there in the storekeeper's words.

'Imagine. All that treasure. Ours, Nathan.'

The sawbones sounded a note of caution. 'We've got to find it first, Larry.'

'Once we find that map, we'll find the treasure. I'm sure of it.'

Jack Strother was alarmed. Map? What map?

Once the doc was out of sight, Strother left cover and hurried along to the saloon where he found Billings the centre of attention, regaling the saloon's patrons with mossy yarns of adventure, prospecting and Indian-fighting. Bradley Creek was a dull town, easily excited, its citizenry mostly made up of men who had spent too many years within its boundaries, and Jethro had the story-teller's ability to make downright lies sound like gospel truth.

'We've got business, Jethro,' Strother said, shoving his way through the considerable crowd, who were willing to replenish the line of one-shot glasses on the bar in front of the old man while he told hair-raising yarn after yarn.

'Right now, Jack?' Billings groaned,

his eyes running along the line of one-shot glasses, the lamp-light above the bar reflected in their amber liquor.

'Right now,' Strother confirmed.

He took the old-timer by the arm and pushed through the crowd, who were none too pleased by his brash action, which robbed them of what promised to be an entertaining interlude to relieve the boredom of small-town life. Jethro grabbed a drink, but a burly, sour-faced man snatched it back.

'No story, no damn drink,' he growled, and tossed the whiskey back in one go.

Outside, Jethro complained.

'You know what, Jack Strother. Being your pard, a man could die of a hellfire thirst for sure.'

Unimpressed by the old-timer's grousing, Strother headed for the livery.

'We can't leave town without supplies, Jack.'

Strother came up short.

'Well, partner, we can wait until morning and ride out with half this damn town dogging our tails, and that's if we see the morning.' Strother's eyes searched the deepening shadows. 'Because we've got a diamond that makes us ripe for killing.'

Jethro accepted Strother's succinct stating of their perilous situation, but said:

'I'd like to see Ike planted decent-like before quitting this burg.'

'We'll do that, Jethro,' Strother stated. 'Right now.'

Strother diverted down an alley that brought them to the rear of the undertaker's. He prised open a window and slipped inside.

'You wait outside,' he told Jethro. There were three bodies covered with sheets, and Strother had the awful feeling that one of them, if not all three, would rise up. Taking deep breaths, he searched for Ike Billings.

'Did you have to be the third,' Strother complained on finding Billings's body. He quickly selected a coffin, a plain wooden box, and put Ike in it. He then levered the coffin out through the open window with Jethro's assistance.

'What now?' Jethro wanted to know, when Strother put in an appearance a couple of seconds later.

'We bury him. There's always an open grave waiting to be filled.'

Their progress to the other end of town, where the cemetery was located, was slow and cautious; they were forced to take cover several times to let citizens pass by and to let Jethro rest up. When at last they reached the graveyard, it was as Strother had said. Just inside the entrance there was an open grave, into which they lowered Ike Billings. Without shovels, they had no option but to scoop as much earth as would cover the coffin into the grave. Their prayers were brief for two reasons, firstly because both men had forgotten most of the prayers they had been taught, and secondly they did not want to risk being seen or heard.

'Ain't nothing fancy, Ike,' Jethro said.

'But it's the best me and Jack can do, and you're going to have to be satisfied with it.' He turned to Strother, who had stepped aside to let Jethro have a private moment with his brother. 'Let's get our nags and shake off the dust of this haunt, partner.'

They were nearing the livery when a whoosh of orange flame burst from its gates.

'The livery's on fire!' the old-timer exclaimed unneccessarily.

'We've got to get our horses out of there, Jethro,' Strother said, breaking into a run. 'Or we're damn well stranded in this burg!'

Watching the burning livery from the infirmary window, Nathan Brandy chuckled gleefully. His visit to the livery, after his chinwag with Saunders the owner of the general store, had been a precaution that had now paid off handsomely. The joint opinion of Larry Saunders and Ben Clane, the owner of the livery, was that Strother and the old-timer would not risk leaving town at night and without supplies, but Brandy's opinion had differed and had proved to be the wiser.

'I reckon Billings hasn't enough brains to fill the eye of a needle,' had been his wisdom. 'But on the brief meeting I had with Strother, I figure that he's got enough brains for them both, and courage too. I think he'll quickly figure out the reason for the general store's closure, and he's smart enough to realize the risk he'd be taking of hanging around town with that great big diamond in his pocket.

'So, all in all, partners,' he had concluded, 'I reckon that Strother will try to slip out of town tonight. And that's where you come in, Clane.'

'How will I stop Strother from leaving?' had been the livery-owner's worry.

The town doctor picked up a fist of straw.

'A livery must be about the easiest and quickest place to set alight,' he'd said. 'I bet if I poured a little kerosene and struck a match, this whole place would be like hell upon earth in minutes.'

'Burn down the livery!' Clane had exclaimed, paling at the thought.

'A small price to pay for that treasure waiting to be collected,' Brandy proposed.

7

By the time Strother and Billings reached the livery, time counted in seconds, the fire was already leaping up the front and sides of the tinder-dry building. Ten minutes at the outside, and the livery would crumble, twenty and it would be smouldering debris. Billings hauled Strother back as he tried to find a niche in the flames through which he could slip.

'That would be a darn loco thing to do, Jack,' he berated Strother. 'There's nothing we can do.'

Strother's face was pained by the whining of the horses inside.

'They're our nags in there, Jethro,' he said grim-faced. 'We can't just let them perish!'

'And what would be the point of perishing with them?' Billings reasoned sensibly.

Strother shook off Jethro's restraint.

'The rear wall hasn't caught yet.' He ran to the back of the burning building.

Having set the fire when he saw Jack Strother and the old-timer making tracks for the livery, Ben Clane now watched from cover as Strother came racing round the building, with Jethro bringing up the rear.

'What are you planning on doing, Jack,' the old-timer asked anxiously.

Strother was testing the rear wall of the livery. 'I'm hoping to find a plank that I can prise loose. And if I can find one, the planks either side shouldn't be too difficult to remove. Maybe that will give me the chance to get the horses out before this whole building collapses.'

Clane gulped. His plan of torching the building and escaping through the rear wall could now backfire and work to Strother's advantage if he found the loose section of wall through which he had made his own escape.

'It's no good, Jack,' Billings said

despairingly, as flames began to lick sections of the rear wall.

There could be little or no time left, but Strother continued frantically to probe the wall. Suddenly, he stopped, not believing his good fortune when a plank moved at his touch. He tested the plank and it slid sideways, as did the planks on either side.

Ben Clane began to sweat. It looked as though Strother might succeed in his plan to rescue the horses. And if that happened, he'd have burned down his livery and be left penniless for no good reason. His hope was momentarily restored when the stiffish breeze that had sprung up was sucked in through the opening in the wall, forcing Strother back. But then the fickle nature of the breeze favoured Strother, and instead of preventing his entrance, the breeze opened up a tunnel through the inferno through which Jack Strother sprinted.

As Strother brought the first horse to safety, panic overcame the livery-keeper. The old-timer calmed the wild-eyed beast, while Strother dashed back into the inferno. Lemon bitter, Clane saw the pot of gold he'd been dreaming of ever since Brandy's and Saunders' visit, slipping from his grasp, leaving him destitute. Then a thought with a slow fuse crept to mind. Why not settle for the fabulous diamond that had started the treasure fever? And to hell with his new-found partners. He'd be long gone before they realized what had happened.

He crept from cover.

Jethro Billings tensed as he felt the point of a knife at his jugular.

'Easy, old man,' Clane murmured. 'I aim to have that diamond. And if I have to slit your windpipe to get it, that's what I'll do.'

The blade nicked his thoat, and Jethro felt a trickle of hot blood.

8

'Ain't got it,' Jethro croaked. 'That di'mond is Jack Strother's. You try and take it from him and he could become real tetchy.'

'Guess it's time to find out,' Clane said, as Strother sprang from the opening in the livery wall just as the fickle breeze changed direction again and the searing fire closed in behind him, chasing him with a curling tongue of flame that almost caught him.

'Well, Jethro,' he said. 'Looks like we're home free, friend.'

'Not quite, Strother.'

Strother dived for his gun.

'I wouldn't do that,' Ben Clane warned, 'if you want the old man to go on living. Unbuckle your gunbelt and toss it over here.'

Silently cursing the euphoria which

had made him careless, Strother did as Clane ordered.

'Sensible,' the livery-keeper said. 'Now, if you'll just hand over the diamond that's got this town worked up so much, Mr Strother, I'll be on my way, no harm done. And if you don't hand over the diamond, I'll cut the old man's thoat from ear to ear.'

'Don't hand it over, Jack,' Jethro said. 'My time is almost used up anyway.'

The commotion in the main street was growing. 'We ain't got much time,' Clane said edgily. 'Are you going to hand over the diamond or not, Strother?'

He yanked back Jethro's head, priming the old man's windpipe for the slash of the knife.

'You can have the diamond!'

'That's a real smart move, mister,' Clane said. 'Hand it over.'

Strother took the rawhide pouch containing the diamond from his trousers pocket and slung it to the livery-owner. The pouch sailed over

Clane. Strother had played crafty. Clane could not let the pouch drop into the darkness, so he'd have to reach for it.

He reached.

Strother leaped through the air, coming down heavily on Clane. However, Clane, fit and muscular from the hard work of running a livery, turned Strother, and when they crashed to the ground he had the upper hand. The point of his knife was only a whisper away from Jack Strother's throat.

9

Strother's hand clasping Clane's knife hand was straining desperately to keep the blade from plunging into his throat. In the mêlée Jethro had been violently tossed aside and, dazed, was no help to Strother. Clane, confident that he could overcome his adversary, grinned wolfishly, pressing home smidgen by smidgen the wicked blade of the hunting knife.

The sound of running feet and shouting on the main street caused the second's distraction that Strother needed, and Clane's fleeting preoccupation gave him the chance to unbalance the livery-owner just enough to spin him aside and reverse their positions.

Strother's fist swung out and crashed forcefully against the side of Clane's head, spinning his eyes. Not wasting a second, he unleashed another haymaker to the other side of the livery-keeper's head. Then, leaping to his feet, he hauled Clane with him and landed a gut-crunching blow to his belly. As Clane folded over, Strother brought his knee up into his face. Ben Clane swayed on legs of jelly like a puppet controlled by a drunk puppeteer. Strother drew back his right arm and sent his fist flying dead centre into Clane's face. Whimpering, the livery-keeper was catapulted back into the dark.

With only seconds to spare, Strother searched frantically for the rawhide pouch containing the diamond. Luckily, the light from the burning livery made his search a brief one. The terrified horses had taken fright. He grabbed the two saddles he had retrieved from the inferno.

'Come on, Jethro,' he said. 'We've got to get those horses back!'

Both men vanished into the night in search of the horses.

By now the livery was collapsing in

on itself. The disintegrating structure served a purpose. The onrushing crowd were forced back, giving Strother and Jethro time to get away. Luckily, the horses had not gone far and were soon saddled. But Strother thought it wiser to wait until the town quietened down before leaving. They hid out in the graveyard, until a degree of calmness was restored.

★ ★ ★

Two hours later, with the commotion over Ben Clane's death, having fallen on his own knife, and the mysterious burning of the livery abating, Sam Cranton, the town marshal, himself wanting to relay to Ben Bradley the happenings in town as quickly as he could, urged folk to let the matter rest until the morning when he promised to instigate a full investigation.

★ ★ ★

Larry Saunders was pacing Nathan Brandy's office, much to his annoyance.

'Settle down, Larry,' he growled impatiently. 'I'm trying to think.'

'What is there to think about?' the owner of the general store grumbled. 'Clane's dead. Strother and the old-timer have lit out. And, frankly, the idea of back-tracking along the wagon trail in the hope of finding that Spaniard's grave and the map in that damned tin box is loco.'

'You thought it was a good enough idea when you first heard it!' Brandy barked. Then, in a more conciliatory tone: 'Look, there's no point in us arguing, Larry. We've still got every chance of getting our hands on the treasure.'

'How do you figure that?' Saunders asked aggressively, giving no quarter to Brandy's attempt to take the heat out of their disagreement.

'Simple.'

'Yeah!'

'Strother and the old man haven't an

idea where Raoul's Treasure is hidden either. If Billings knew, do you think he'd be living off crumbs?'

Saunder's spirits brightened. 'You're right.'

'Any one of a hundred canyons could be Devil's Canyon. And that was the Apaches' name for it anyway. And even if the canyon is the one that that old reprobate Billings thinks it is, they've still got to find the treasure. It isn't going to be sitting out in the open waiting to be picked up. That's what there's a map for.'

Saunders calmed.

'First light and we hit the trail, Larry.'

*   *   *

'Want me to intervene in the gentlemen's departure, m'lady?'

Cecily Lyle-Hackett turned from her hotel bedroom window from where she was watching Jack Strother and Jethro's departure, having guessed correctly that he would not try to leave while the town was in an uproar. She paced the room restlessly, considering Bambridge's proposition. When she stopped pacing, her face was full of resolve.

'No, Bambridge. I've got a better idea.'

'As always, m'lady,' the manservant complimented.

*　*　*

Another interested spectator of Strother's and Billings's departure was Marshal Sam Cranton. Though he had figured that the burning down of the livery and Ben Clane's death was tied in with Strother and Billings and Raoul's Treasure, he had not run himself ragged trying to find them, because he wanted them to leave town safely. A curious man by nature, and a cautious man by profession, instinct had him listening outside the infirmary window, where he had overheard Jack Strother and Jethro Billings talking. It had been a conversation that had sent his pulse racing.

Cranton's first instinct was to act alone. He had a half-baked plan of following Strother and the old-timer, and then waylaying them when they found Raoul's Treasure. But he soon saw the dangers inherent in that idea. And it was then that he had decided to share his knowledge with Ben Bradley. He had the resources, both human and mechanical, to secure the treasure. Better a piece of the pie than no pie at all, Cranton had wisely decided.

Once Strother and Billings were out of sight, and riding low in the saddle to up his pace, he lost no time in arriving in the Bradley yard.

Ben Bradley entered the den of the ranch house, hollow-eyed from drowning his sorrows, having been sent packing by the English woman.

'What do you want?' he enquired sourly of Cranton.

'There's been hellish excitement in town, Ben,' the marshal said. 'I figured you'd want to know.'

'Excitement? What kind of excitment would that be, Cranton?'

★   ★   ★

With a swift chop to the back of the neck, precisely delivered and efficiently executed, Bambridge effortlessly relieved the two late revellers leaving the saloon of their horses.

'Sorry, gentlemen,' he apologized to the unconscious cowboys. 'But the restoration to respectability of the Lyle-Hacketts is at stake.'

He led the horses to the rear of the hotel, to where Cecily Lyle-Hackett had made her way by the hotel fire escape, not having bothered to pay the bill, a not uncommon ocurrence.

'The best I could do at such short notice, m'lady,' the manservant apologized, when her ladyship looked disapprovingly at the jaded nags.

'I'll probably have flea bites every-where,' she complained.

'Might I sincerely suggest to your ladyship that, during the ordeal of having to ride these — as our American friends would say — *critters*, that you keep the possible reward for your discomfort in mind to assuage your distress.'

Cecily Lady-Hackett laughed.

'What would I do without you, Bambridge?'

He smiled. 'What indeed, m'lady.'

★   ★   ★

'Raoul's Treasure?'

'Yes, Ben,' Sam Cranton enthused. 'More gold and jewels than you ever thought existed.'

Bradley sloshed whiskey into a crystal tumbler and drank it in one gulp.

'That, Cranton,' he growled, 'is the greatest load of horse-shit I've ever heard.'

'Then why is everyone trying to get their mitts on it, Ben?'

'Everyone? Who's everyone?'

108

'Doc Brandy. Larry Saunders. Ben Clane, too. Because I reckon that he torched his own livery with Strother's and the old-timer's nags inside, to try and stop them leaving town. And, of course, there's Lady Lyle-Hackett.'

Ben Bradley's attention was instant.

'Cecily believes this mossy yarn about Raoul's Treasure?'

'Saw her sitting like a hen with an egg at her hotel room window, waiting for Strother and the old-timer to make tracks.'

The rancher became thoughtful.

'You know, Cranton, if her *ladyship* is interested, then this Raoul's Treasure might just exist. Because she's a real foxy lady, is Cecily Lyle-Hackett.'

*   *   *

A couple of miles outside Bradley Creek, Jethro spoke up.

'Figure we got clean away, Jack?' he asked.

'Sure we did, Jethro,' Strother lied, seeing no point in worrying the old-timer before he needed to worry. Which he would have good cause to before very long, Strother reckoned.

10

At first light, Doc Brandy and Larry Saunders set out along the old wagon trail over which Saunders had travelled to Bradley Creek; a trail long since abandoned in favour of shorter trails over which a man could make quicker progress. With the tentacles of law and order reaching out into every corner of the West in the shape of US marshals, tough-hided and long-riding sheriffs and marshals, a lot of men needed to make fast tracks.

'I hope you're reckoning right on this one, Nathan,' Saunders fretted. 'Maybe we should have tracked Strother and the old-timer like that English lady and her manservant.' It was a much repeated statement through a long day, in which every second seemed like an hour.

'Trust me, Larry,' Brandy said. 'It's a big country. Strother and Billings will probably search until they drop and never get near the treasure. But with a map, we can go right to the exact spot where this fella Raoul stashed it.'

'If we find the map, that is,' Saunders grumbled.

Brandy turned his face away. The last thing he needed was for the storekeeper to see worry drawing the lines of his face tight. Placing his trust in Saunder's recognizing where the Spaniard who had travelled on the wagon train with him was buried, was a long shot that could pan out either way. But he consoled himself with the thought that tagging along after Strother and the old-timer was an equally uncertain long shot. The only advantage to be gained, had he opted for that, would be the chance of getting his hands on the diamond. He was beginning to regret that he had not settled for possession of the fabulous stone by killing Strother and the old-timer back in town. Or by bushwhacking them outside the town. The problem with that course of action was the awful risk involved. Not being gun-handy, he would have had to rely on stealth — a precisely wielded knife across the throat or in the gut. But cowardice had made him rethink that plan. Because if it had failed, he had no doubt but that Strother would have wreaked a terrible revenge.

It had surprised Brandy that he had a larcenous and killer streak in him. He had made up his mind that he would kill if necessary to get his hands on Raoul's Treasure. He was a medical man, trained to save life and live upright, and he had never thought other than that would be the way of it to the grave. However, when his gaze had rested on the diamond, something inside him went spinning awry, and from out of a dark corner of his mind another man emerged; a man who was a greedy and ruthless killer. And now he reckoned that, whether he got his hands on Raoul's Treasure or not, he could never again be the man he had been.

Late in the evening, well along the old wagon trail, Saunders drew rein and let his eyes roam over the flat plain.

'Is this where the Spaniard was buried?' Brandy asked eagerly.

For a spell, Saunders continued to look.

'Well, is it or isn't it!' the sawbones demanded.

★　★　★

Having learned his craft in India, Bambridge was an excellent tracker and read sign as good as any Apache. He stood up from a close examination of what, to Cecily Lyle-Hacket, looked like squiggles in the sandy soil.

'We're on track, your ladyship,' he announced confidently. 'Mr Strother is making an admirable attempt at disguising his passage. I would hazard a guess that he has tied a swish to his horse's tail to draw after him to obliterate his tracks. But such old native tricks were commonplace in India and other parts of the Empire where I had the privilege to serve.'

He mounted up.

'We must quicken our pace, m'lady. Mr Strother has opened up a considerable lead, I fear.' Leading off, he added; 'I do hope your ladyship is not suffering too much distress.'

'Regardless of my discomfort, we must press on, Bambridge.'

'Good show, m'lady!'

*　*　*

Jack Strother was no fool, and neither was Jethro Billings.

'You keep looking behind you all the time, and your head will fall off,' was the old-timer's comment, when again Strother checked his back trail. 'You've been dancing that horse round like a Sally at a barn dance. But you ain't fooling me none, Jack Strother, with all that guff about me and you having nothing to worry about. We'll attract attention like shit attracts flies!' He drew rein. 'So tell me what you're seeing back there.'

'Nothing. Yet,' Strother said.

'But we've got company, right?'

'I figure,' Strother said.

'Any idea who?'

'Take your pick, Jethro. I figure that the doc and the storekeeper won't rest in town. And then there's the crooked marshal of Bradley Creek, Sam Cranton. I reckon he'll tell Ben Bradley about the treasure. And, of course, there'll be Lady Lyle-Hackett.'

Strother groaned. 'And bandits, too.'

'Bandits?' Jethro asked.

'Yeah,' Strother sighed. 'Mex bandits. Like the ones watching us right now, Jethro.'

11

The old-timer swung about in his saddle to look at the ridge behind him. His breath caught in his throat when he saw at least twenty riders.

'What do we do?' he asked urgently.

'Not much we can do, Jethro. I figure a hand is about to be dealt, and there's no point in doing a thing until we see the cards.'

'*Amigo*!' the bandit leader hailed. 'You wait. We talk.'

'They'll cut our throats,' Jethro gulped. 'Let's run for it, Jack.'

'And how far do you figure you'd get with at least twenty rifles spitting lead at you, Jethro?'

'Way I see it, is that we'd be better running chickens than sitting ducks!'

Strother grabbed hold of Billings's reins to stop him bolting.

The bandits were making their way

down a steep shale track off the ridge, some of them fighting to stay in the saddle, others riding with the ease and expertise of a lifetime with their butts in leather and their boots in stirrups.

'I gotta run for it, Jack!' the old-timer gasped. 'That cut-throat's name is Eduardo Sanchez.' On hearing the bandit leader's name, Jack Strother shifted uneasily in his saddle. Sanchez's reputation for evil doings rivalled the devil's. 'He had a brother, Pablo, a critter uglier than a vulture.'

'Heard he got his come-uppance down near the border.'

'Yeah, he did. I killed him.'

'Why the hell didn't you say so, Jethro!'

'I've been darn well trying to. But you've got ears that don't hear so well!'

Strother looked to the line of *bandidos* making their way down the steep shale trail, the more experienced front riders almost at the end of the trail.

'Ride like hell, Jethro!' he yelled,

already sinking spurs.

'Now it's all hurry, ain't it,' the old-timer groused, quickly catching up and setting the pace for Strother to match.

'Where the hell did you learn to ride like this, Jethro?' was Strother's shouted enquiry.

'By having angry husbands and Mex bandits on my tail. That's how.'

At the start of their dash the air was filled with confused and surprised voices. Now that had changed to the buzz of angry gunfire, as the air around and over them hummed with flying lead.

★　★　★

Larry Saunders wandered about the plain where he figured the wagon train Spaniard was buried. Nathan Brandy dogged his every footstep, much to his annoyance.

'Well,' the Bradley Creek sawbones pressed Saunders impatiently. 'Is this the place or not?'

'I'm looking,' Saunders flung back tetchily. 'It's all this tall grass.'

Brandy looked out across the sea of waving grass.

Suddenly, the storekeeper cut loose with a wild yell, startling Brandy, the sawbones fearing that the heat had boiled Saunders' brain. The yell curled back like a ghost answering, an acoustic peculiar to the place where the Spaniard had been planted for his misdeeds.

'This is the place, Nathan,' Saunders stated positively. 'I recall how sound did this crazy loop where the Spaniard was buried.' He grinned. 'A couple of the women the Spaniard had been pleasuring took to caterwauling like banshees scaring folk plenty I can tell you.'

'I'm not interested in cute tales, Saunders,' Brandy rebuked him. 'Just find the Spaniard's damn grave! Where are you going?' he questioned a minute later, when it seemed to him that the storekeeper went marching off.

'Back to the trail.' Saunders pointed. 'See that tree over there. The Irishman's wagon was just about there when the Spaniard was caught with his lady's delight where it had no good reason to be, and directly in line with where he planted the Spaniard. About fifty feet or so off the trail, I reckon.'

'Well, start counting.'

Nathan Brandy excitedly shoved the store owner ahead of him.

★   ★   ★

Ben Bradley gave his men the order to change to the second string of fresh horses they had in tow. Playing catch up, they had ridden their mounts hard. His criticism of Sam Cranton's eager departure from Bradley Creek to bring him the news of Raoul's Treasure had been barbed.

'Didn't it occur to you, Cranton,' he had railed, 'that you should have followed Strother to see in which direction he was headed. Then we wouldn't have to ride our asses raw and good horses to a standstill trying to pick up his trail.'

Hearing it as Bradley told it, Cranton could see the mistake he had made in his haste to ingratiate himself with the rancher.

In the saddle, on the new mounts, the relentless pace was renewed over trail after trail.

'We're runnin' round like headless chickens, Mr Bradley,' one of the men protested.

Bradley shot him.

'Has anyone else got a gripe?' he snarled. Muteness was the crew's response.

'Guessed you wouldn't have,' he taunted.

Sam Cranton suddenly wished that he was back in Bradley Creek, safe and well. That he had gone to bed the night before, and had never ridden out to the the Bradley ranch. Ben Bradley, driven by the prospect of colossal riches, was mean enough to drop any man who stood in his way. The harsh ride and the scorching heat would fray tempers. And the more edgy the men became, the greater the threat of sudden and violent danger would become. There was one man already dead. And there could be a whole lot more.

Cranton glumly knew that he was sitting on a powder-keg, needing only a spark.

★ ★ ★

Bambridge was unexpectedly stumped. He was looking at several trails leading in different directions, but which was the genuine one? Jack Strother was a very clever man. He had set up several false trails.

'What is it, Bambridge?' Cecily Lyle-Hackett questioned, impatient with what she saw as time-wasting.

A proud man, Bambridge did not want to admit to his confusion.

'Just making sure that we're on the right track, m'lady.'

'Well be quick about it!'

'Yes, your ladyship.' He had always been a lucky man, having survived many battles serving in the far flung corners of the British Empire. So he prayed now that his luck would serve him well again. He mounted up.

'This way your ladyship,' he said.

'Are you quite sure, Bambridge?'

'Oh, yes, your ladyship,' he replied, with a confidence he was far from feeling.

* * *

'Never knew so many bullets had been made,' Jethro Billings griped, as the hail of lead buzzing around him from the *bandidos*' guns continued.

Strother glanced behind him. They had opened up a sizeable gap between them and Sanchez's cut-throats, but he knew that it was down to the fact that the bandits had chosen to use lead instead of horse in pursuit of their revenge. But that was about to change,

Eduardo Sanchez was organizing his riders, and soon the sizeable gap would be a much reduced gulf. That was, of course, if the lead-thickened air did not rain down on them first.

Strother had one more problem; a problem Jethro shared. Tired horses, which were fast losing their wind.

★　★　★

'Forty ... Forty one ... Forty two ... ' Larry Saunders counted off the paces to where he reckoned the Spaniard was buried. Nathan Brandy followed eagerly behind, carrying the brand-new shovels from the general store. Deciding, the storekeeper stamped his foot on the ground.

'Let's dig right here, Nathan,' he said.

12

Jack Strother's big worry was, that in country he was not familiar with, he could be riding into more trouble than he was riding away from. So when Jethro shouted: 'Cut into the canyon ahead,' he was left with no choice but to trust the old-timer's superior — he hoped — geographical knowledge. But his experience with canyons was not happy, having a time or two ridden into ones that ended in a solid wall of rock, or presented a myriad of trails that confused a man so much that he was left chasing his own rear end.

'Is there a way out of this canyon, Jethro?' he yelled, above the whine of lead and the thunder of hoofs.

'Sure there is,' Billings said, but Strother had a niggling feeling about the old man's cocky confidence.

What troubled him most about Jethro

Billings was his penchant for dealing out the real story and true facts piecemeal. But with Sanchez and his cutthroats close enough now for him to hear their swearing and threats, his options were zero. He had to trust Jethro. And that fact filled him with trepidation.

They thundered into the mouth of the canyon. Sanchez, howling louder than a shot-in-the-ass coyote for their blood, followed hot on their heels.

★   ★   ★

'How many more damn holes are we going to have to dig?'

Saunders, as spent as Brandy, looked at the doc's scowling face.

'How the hell do I know,' he said. He stabbed at the newly turned earth. 'All I know is that if we want to find that Spaniard's grave, we've got to keep digging.'

The Bradley Creek sawbones looked around him at the dozen or so holes they had already dug, his shoulders drooping in despair. They could dig up the entire plain, and not find what they were looking for. Maybe, he thought despondently, they weren't even in the right place.

Saunders went rigid as his shovel unearthed a tooth.

'Doc,' he said quietly, showing him the shovel of earth and the tooth therein. 'As I recall that Spainard had real fine gnashers. It was his smile that first got the ladies' interest.' He chuckled. 'After that it was other parts of him that held it.'

For a breathless moment, both men stood entranced by the tooth, before they resumed frenzied digging. Great shovels of black earth were cast left and right of the deepening hole in the ground, until they came to a further amazed halt. Poking out of the earth, they saw a human skull with a hole between its eye-sockets, where the Irishman, whose woman the Spaniard had been caught pleasuring, had shot him.

There followed even more frenzied digging for the tin box holding the map which would pinpoint the location of Raoul's Treasure.

*   *   *

Just when Bambridge was getting dizzy from, he suspected, going around in circles, and was ready to confess to her ladyship that they might not be on the right trail, the sound of gunfire made him hold his tongue and hope that a reprieve was in the offing.

'If you wouldn't mind waiting, m'lady,' he said, 'while I seek out the source of this gunfire and its threat to your ladyship's well-being, and ascertain its purpose.'

He dismounted and took from his saddlebag a brass spyglass, a souvenir taken from the body of a Georgian charlatan who had offended Lady Lyle-Hackett by suggesting that she should, as he had so crudely put it, *open her goddam English legs for him.*

'Do be careful, Bambridge,' Cecily Lyle-Hackett urged, as he began to climb a steep track up to the highest point of the terrain.

'So kind of you to concern yourself, m'lady,' he said, genuinely pleased that she should care.

Cecily Lyle-Hackett's concern was not wholly for the manservant. Her worry was also that were anything to happen Bambridge, she would be alone in a heathen, uncivilized land, at the mercy of predators both human, animal and reptile.

Bambridge climbed swiftly, showing his Scottish Highland roots, strong of limb and straight of back. His only concession to caution was the removal of his bowler hat when he reached the summit of the higher ground and peered over its rim. He could see two men being chased by at least twenty. He put the spyglass to his right eye, and saw Jack Strother and Jethro Billings riding hell-for-leather for their lives. The overwhelming odds against the duo made his spirits flag. He saw no chance of their survival, which in turn meant that the treasure was lost.

'Well, what is it, Bambridge?' Cecily Lyle-Hackett quizzed him impatiently on his return. 'You look rather glum.'

'With good reason, m'lady,' he intoned drearily. 'Sadly, it seems that Mr Strother and Mr Billings have rather a short time to live.'

13

Had Jack Strother been within earshot, he'd have whole-heartedly concurred with Bambridge's assessment of his and Jethro's desperate plight. A quick glance over his shoulder told him that the bandits were gaining ground fast, and there wasn't a damn thing he could do about it; his horse's wind was running out and it showed in the mare's loping gait as the energy drained from her legs. She could fold any second now.

As he pulled away, it was obvious that Jethro Billings had the better horse.

'Keep that nag going, Jack,' he shouted. 'If this is the canyon I figure it is, it's got a hidy-hole that'll fool those bastards.' He added a warning: 'But we've got to get inside the canyon with a clear lead.'

'I'm doing my damn best, Jethro,' Jack Strother flung back. 'But if this nag folds, you keep right on going, you hear?'

'Hah! Ain't never figured otherwise, Jack.'

'Thanks, *partner*,' Strother called back sarcastically. He coaxed the mare. 'Come on, gal. You can do it for old Jack Strother, honey.'

★　★　★

Ben Bradley was on his fifth different trail and rattler-mean, when he picked up sign — Strother's, he hoped.

'I reckon I'm going to be a very rich man, Cranton,' he laughed crazily.

'Sure you are, Ben,' the Bradley Creek marshal humoured the rancher, fearing the loco light in the rancher's eyes, and the backlash it would bring to the man who would be stupid enough to buck him. As yet, Bradley had not spotted the three men who had taken their chance to drop out. And the lackey-lawman prayed that by the time he did, Ben Bradley would have his hands on Raoul's Treasure to sweeten his nature, or there would be hell to pay.

* * *

'We must do something, Bambridge,' Cecily Lyle-Hackett urged the man-servant, having climbed to the top of the rise from where Bambridge had observed Strother's and Billings's perilous situation. It shocked Bambridge to see her ladyship clawing her way up the rise with the abandon of a common person. And as a result, ending up grimied and dishevelled like a woman of infinitely lower class. He was not used to such behaviour in the aristocracy, and he hoped that her ladyship had but taken leave of her senses on this single ocassion.

'I could try a rifle shot for you, m'lady,' Bambridge said. 'Though what beneficial result it would have evades me.'

'Well, get on with it, Bambridge,' she

commanded, unwilling to debate the merits or demerits of the outcome.

Having learned in India and other outposts of Empire that hurried action usually ended in an unsatisfactory outcome, he settled himself with great care before putting the rifle sights to his right eye.

'Oh, do get on with it!' Cecily Lyle-Hackett urged.

Bambridge was of the opinion, as he had been since shortly after their arrival in America, and particularly its Western reaches, that her ladyship's standards were being tainted by the unsalubrious nature of that society, if the melange of breeds that made up America could even be remotely called *society*.

Picking his target, he pulled the trigger. The rifle bucked, but its recoil was not as severe as the English rifle he had been used to. Having allowed for the more robust recoil of the British soldier's rifle, his first shot fell harmlessly wide of the mark. But it did have the effect of slowing the riders.

'Shoot again,' Cecily Lyle-Hackett ordered. 'And this time make it count, Bambridge.'

'I shall, of course, do my best as always to please your ladyship.'

Sanchez and his men were swinging about in their saddles to try and pinpoint the shooter, when a second shot rang out and the man nearest to the outlaw leader toppled from his saddle.

'By jove, well done, Bambridge,' Cecily Lyle-Hackett enthused, dancing excitedly. Bambridge pulled her down alongside him. 'What on earth do you think you're doing,' she berated him. 'How dare you, Bambridge!'

'I am most profoundly sorry, m'lady,' he profusely apologized. 'But it would be unwise to let those vile and unwholesome individuals see you. Were that to happen, I'd fear the turn of ill-fortune it would precipitate.'

Cecily Lyle-Hackett, of course, saw the wisdom of his action. But, as the Americans would so succinctly put it, she'd be damned if she'd admit it!

'Really, Bambridge, you must be more restrained in your behaviour,' she said, with just the right degree of aristocratic haughtiness. It would never do for a servant, even of Bambridge's long and loyal service, much of it unpaid service in recent times, to get above his station.

★   ★   ★

Jack Strother did not know who had shot the bandit, nor did he care. He simply accepted his good fortune. The shooting had brought Eduardo Sanchez and his cut-throats up short, which gave Strother and Jethro vital minutes to widen the gap between them and the *bandidos*, to open up the lead they needed to gain the safe refuge of the hidy-hole. Strother sincerely hoped that there *was* a hidy-hole. That it was not another Billings tall tale.

On entering the canyon a short distance behind Jethro, Jack Strother's spirits were raised by the old man's purposeful ride along a narrow trail with which he seemed to be familiar. Soon, the trail narrowed to a track running between two towering rockfaces, barely wide enough for their horses to pass along. When Jethro drew rein, frowning, on facing a web of trails like the veins on the back of a man's hands, Jack Strother's heart flipped over.

'Darn,' Jethro sighed. 'It's been a while, Jack. And then, maybe, this ain't the canyon I thought it was in the first place.' He scratched his stubbled chin, pondering his options. 'Got a nickel?'

'A nickel?'

'To flip. Tails, we go thataway,' he pointed straight ahead. 'And heads we — '

'Jethro,' Strother bellowed. 'I ain't never murdered a man before, but I might in the next couple of seconds!'

* * *

'Give it here!' Nathan Brandy grabbed the rusted tin box that Larry Saunders was trying to prise open. However, Brandy's attempt to open the box proved every bit as unsuccessful as the store-keeper's.

'Get a rock. We'll smash it open.'

'Be careful you don't damage the map,' Saunders cautioned, as Brandy was about to drop the sizeable rock on the rusted and fragile tin box. The sides of the box split open. Both men stood aghast at what they found.

★   ★   ★

Eduardo Sanchez dispatched three riders in the only direction from where a man could shoot unseen: the rise of ground to the east. He then spurred his horse to resume his pursuit of the *Americanos*, one of which, the older of the pair, he remembered. He would skin the old man inch by inch for killing his brother Pablo.

★   ★   ★

'Come on,' Strother ordered Jethro Billings, taking the lead.

'This might not be the right track, Jack,' the old-timer cautioned. 'A mistake now, and we're done for, for sure.'

'When you're holding cards not worth a spit, you pray, Jethro.'

'Then I'm praying, Jack.'

'Yeah,' Strother said, on hearing Sanchez and his henchmen thunder into the canyon. 'This might be the time to renew your acquaintance with your Maker, sure enough.'

Strother coaxed the exhausted mare into one last effort. The track was a dead end. Strother looked at the solid rockface ahead. There had been no time to cover their tracks, which meant that Sanchez and his hardcases were coming right to their door.

'I'll be damned, Jack Strother!' Jethro yelled and galloped past him, intending, it seemed, to ride straight into the rockface.

It looked to Jack Strother as though Jethro Billings had at last lost his wits.

14

'Only half the map,' Saunders said, stunned.

'And that's about as useful as one hand to a piano player,' Nathan Brandy growled. 'We've got to keep digging, there must be another box.'

Saunders looked to the scorching sun.

'Keep digging?' Exhausted, he leaned heavily on his shovel. 'I ain't got the spit to lift a blade of grass.'

Brandy began frantically scooping earth from the hole.

'It's here, and I'm going to find it,' he said grimly, shovelling earth even more frantically.

'Mebbe that gent from Barcelona never had no second box, Nathan.' Brandy stopped digging, horror haunting his wan features. 'What if he just kept the second part of the map in his head? I only ever saw one tin box.'

Slowly, Brandy's fears slipped away.

'Why would he keep half the map in a damn tin box and the other half in his head, Larry? Why wouldn't he simply keep the entire map in his head?' Saunders was stumped, but Brandy did not enjoy his cocky confidence for long.

'What if this fella from Barcelona only had half the map, because he was meeting up with someone who had the other half?' suggested the storekeeper. 'Or he was searching for the other half?'

Now it was Nathan Brandy's turn to be stumped, but his reaction was killer-mean. He drew his sixgun and levelled it at Saunders. 'Pick up your damn shovel and start digging,' he ordered stonily. 'Or I'll drop you where you stand.'

After his initial shock, Saunders relaxed and chuckled.

'You ain't no killer, Nathan.' Then, looking into Brandy's frenzied eyes he was shocked at what he saw. The Bradley Creek doctor had indeed become a killer. He began digging.

'You take it easy now, Nathan, you hear. Your finger is real twitchy on that trigger.'

'You just keep right on digging, Saunders,' the sawbones snarled.

After a spell of rapid shovel work, the storekeeper, near spent, complained, 'Ain't you going to help?'

Brandy's response was dogged. 'Just keep digging!'

★   ★   ★

Jack Strother rubbed his eyes and looked again, when Jethro Billings rode into the solid rockface and vanished from sight. A second later he reappeared.

'Come on, Jack,' he called, and added a stern rebuke, 'This ain't no time for dithering.'

With the sound of pursuit getting closer by the second, the old-timer's impatience was warranted. Strother clipped it after Jethro, and on reaching the spot where the old man had miraculously melted into the rockface he spotted a narrow opening, set at an angle that hid it from casual view. The entrance to the small cave barely allowed for a horse and rider to squeeze through. With Strother, like Billings, lean times had made for lean frames, and right then as he slid through the angled aperture in the rockface, Jack Strother saw his sparse times as a blessing.

When he saw Strother glancing behind him at the bandits galloping into the small basin in front of the rockface, Jethro reassured him.

'If you don't know this cave is here, chances are the only way you'll find it is by sheer luck.' Strother's mare was restless. 'Or plain stupidity,' the old-timer snapped. 'Calm the nag.'

Strother calmed the horse, but he wondered for how long. The cave was intensely dark, and filled with slithering sounds.

Billings snorted.

'You ain't scared of a coupla rattlers and their cousins, are you? A man's got to go sometime, Jack. What will be will be, I say.'

Strother figured that if he were as long in the tooth and had had as many adventures and lovers as the old man, he might be a tad philosophical too. But he was at least thirty years Jethro Billings's junior, with, he hoped, a lot of adventures to come. And he hoped even more fervently, a lot of lovers to come, too.

'You know, Jethro, you sure do talk a lot of horse-shit!' Strother growled.

'Gets that way as you get older, Jack. Because all that's left is talking through your rear end, and pretending that you don't mind dying. And,' the years rolled back in Jethro Billings's eyes, 'you start to think that maybe you could have done things different, and maybe better too.'

The dust stirred by the bandits' horses drifted into the cave, so close were they to its opening. Strother held his breath when one of the bandits, a young keen-eyed *hombre* seemed to peer right into the cave, but then looked away.

'Where did the gringos go, Pedro?' he asked a fellow bandit, who was as mystified as the questioner. He crossed himself. 'You think maybe we've been chasing ghosts, *compadre*?'

'Hah! There is no such thing as ghosts, Miguel,' the older bandit said. 'You talk foolish talk, *mi amigo*.'

'Then where have the gringos gone?' Miguel insisted, his eyes wild.

The older man shrugged.

'Of one thing I am certain, Miguel. They have not vanished into thin air.'

There were angrily shouted orders from Sanchez. With the smattering of Mex lingo that Strother had, along with the little Jethro knew, it looked like Sanchez was ordering his men to spread out and search every inch of the canyon and, for good measure, to turn every rock.

Strother, still conscious of what

might be slithering on the floor of the cave or hanging in the darkness from its roof, had another worry added — foul air. They were sharing what little air the small cave possessed with a posse of critters who seemed to like the smell of their own excrement.

'I sure hope that Sanchez will soon tire of his search, Jethro,' he said, barely daring to breathe.

The old-timer sniffed the air.

'It ain't so bad, Jack,' he said. ''Specially when a fella ain't had a bath for five years.'

'Five years!'

'Well, I've been in the desert for most of that time. Water's been too scarce to waste on bathing.'

'So how come all those women kept falling for you, Jethro?' Strother snorted.

The old man puffed out his narrow chest.

'Good old Jethro charm, I guess.'

'Did you ever think that they were just overcome?' Strother speculated.

Jethro sniffed himself. 'Darn,' he

admitted, 'maybe they were at that, Jack.' His smile was a leery one. 'But once they were down, it was sure enjoyable.'

★ ★ ★

'What now, Bambridge?' Cecily Lyle-Hacket asked her manservant, frowning worriedly at the prospect of the oncoming bandits' imminent arrival.

'We shall have to stand and fight, of course, m'lady,' was Bambridge's matter-of-fact response. 'It's the British way.'

Lady Lyle-Hackett was all for the *British way*, but in a more civilized manner. Her talents for survival, which she had exercised with admirable cunning since the Lyle-Hackett fortunes had so dramatically changed due to her idiot father's fondness for fast women and slow horses, were of the more subtle kind. Not for her pistols at dawn, or at any other time if at all possible.

Bambridge completed his assessment of the oncoming riders.

'I very much regret, m'lady, but I fear that I shall have to impose upon your generosity,' he said apologetically.

'What the devil are you talking about, Bambridge?' Cecily Lyle-Hackett asked tetchily. 'Do make sense, there's a good chap.'

'You see, the thing is,' Bambridge went on, 'I am confident that I shall be able to dispatch two of those foul creatures myself by way of my bowler-hat and a makeshift sling-shot, a weapon I became extremely proficient with in the mountain passes of Kashmir while serving the Empire in my small and humble way. This aid to our survival, I shall be able to manufacture from my personal accoutrements. But it may require m'lady's assistance to finish off the third man.'

'My assistance, Bambridge?'

'If your ladyship would oblige?'

'What is it you want me to do?'

'Please forgive me for what I am

about to say, m'lady. But I would wish you to act in a manner befitting a lady of ill-repute.'

Cecily Lyle-Hackett's eyes popped.

'I should say not, Bambridge!'

With the craftiness of the serving classes, who were always careful to let their master or mistress labour under the illusion that they were in command, Bambridge sighed heavily.

'That is a pity, your ladyship.'

He said no more, inviting Cecily Lyle-Hackett to ask:

'What is a pity, Bambridge?'

'Why, that fabulous treasure going to waste, of course, m'lady.' Gotcha cobber, he thought, when the rose in Cecily Lyle-Hackett's English rose complexion began to fade to a colour somewhere between grey and yellow. 'But we did have a jolly good try at getting our hands on it, did we not, m'lady?'

'All right, Bambridge. I shall do as you ask, but under the most severe protest. And you are sworn to secrecy about this affair. Understood?'

'As always, m'lady. My lips are sealed,' he suavely reassured his mistress.

'And I shall, of course, need some instruction to successfully portray the type of lady in question.'

'That goes without saying, m'lady.'

'We can't let it get about that a Lyle-Hackett didn't do her bit, eh, Bambridge.'

'Good show, m'lady.' The manservant came swiftly to attention and saluted.

'Oh, do get on with it, Bambridge,' she scolded him. 'We haven't all the time in the world, you know.'

Bambridge went and draped himself with abandon on a boulder, in a wide-legged pose.

'Good grief!' Cecily Lyle-Hackett exclaimed. 'That, Bambridge, is postively harlotish!'

'Unfortunately, m'lady, your posture must have the kind of' — Bambridge gave a gentle cough — 'whorish nature to scatter the first man's wits.'

He explained.

'From what I have observed, these gentlemen are Mexicans. Therefore, it is to be assumed that they are Latin hot-blooded creatures, of no great social standing, who would react in a manner befitting their kind on glimpsing m'lady's . . . ah . . . ' another gentle cough, 'considerable womanly charms.'

'Bambridge,' Cecily Lyle-Hackett said with all the haughtiness of 500 years of breeding, 'I must warn you that you have stepped outside the bounds of what is acceptable.'

'Yes, m'lady.' Once more he played on her desire to see the Lyle-Hackett fortunes restored, which had been the whole purpose of coming to America in the first place, and which he wished for as fervently as she. 'What I ask of you is reprehensible in the extreme, m'lady, and therefore it would be best to forget about this treasure we seek.'

'You don't fool me, you old rogue,' Cecily Lyle-Hackett said. 'You know very well that I'd sell my soul to possess

Raoul's Treasure.'

'Then if your ladyship would oblige,' he urged. 'The vagabonds are almost upon us.' He took a derringer from his vest pocket and handed it to Cecily Lyle-Hackett. 'It doesn't look much, m'lady. But close up it has its disabling qualities. Together, we should have no problem dealing with these inferiors.'

The manservant quickly assembled his makeshift slingshot, and then climbed to the rocks above the narrow entrance to their hideaway. He took off his steel-rimmed bowler-hat, which he readied to use in his practised deadly fashion.

★   ★   ★

'More gringos, Señor Sanchez!'

Jack Strother heard the bandit's yell, and the shuffling of horses in reponse to the outlaw's warning cry. His hope was that Eduardo Sanchez's concentration on finding him and Jethro would be redirected. His hopes were realized.

'Ride!' Sanchez ordered. 'We will show the filthy gringos who are masters.'

'I guess we're off the hook, Jack,' Jethro said.

'And just in the nick of time, Jethro,' Strother answered, gagging. 'You sit tight.' He left the cave with the caution of a fox raiding a hen-house, choking on the cloud of swirling dust stirred up by the bandits' urgent departure.

'Well?' Jethro enquired tensely from within the cave.

'Looks like we're home free, Jethro,' he replied, just before a bullet whipped his hat off.

15

Grabbing his rifle, Jack Strother leaped from his horse for the protection of nearby rocks, bandit lead a constant and deadly threat. He cursed his carelessness. He should have known that the wily Eduardo Sanchez would have left men behind. And that was what came from Yanqui perception that Mexicans were dumbheads.

Cocooned in the rocks, Strother scanned the higher reaches of the canyon, and spotted the glint of sunlight on a rifle barrel. How many men had Sanchez left behind? And how the hell could he dislodge them? They had an eagle's perch, and any attempt by him to reach them could only end in his demise. He couldn't expect any help from Jethro; the old-timer would not have anything near the stamina it would take to work his way up through the rocks to the Mexicans' lair.

'Jack,' Jethro called out. 'You OK?'

'So far, Jethro,' Strother called back.

'How many of the critters?'

'Can't be sure.'

'I'm coming out.'

'No. You stay put!' Strother commanded.

'Damned if I will,' the old man shouted back. 'Cover me, Jack!'

⋆   ⋆   ⋆

'Holy shit!' Ben Bradley swore, when he saw the bandits riding at full stretch towards them, guns blazing. 'Mex bandits! Take cover,' he hollered.

The Bradley crew looked around at the flat, arid terrain.

'Cover?' an angry man bellowed. 'What damn cover?'

There was a rise of ground to the east, where Sanchez had dispatched riders to root out whoever had shot at them, but the bandits had cleverly cut off that possible escape route. They were outnumbered by at least two to one, and in the main were men who were used to nursing cows and doing the chores of ranching, not gun-feuding. They packed guns, but in most cases used them to hammer nails into broken fences, except on the odd time when they fired shots over the head of an interloper on the Bradley range. The range wars, when a man's skill with a pistol was more important than his roping and wrangling skills, were over with some years ago; years in which ranch-owners' priorities had changed, and any man hired needed to know more about cows than night raids and mayhem.

But, to judge by the skill of the bandits' shooting, their refinement and civilizing had a long way to go to catch up with their *Americano* neighbours. Four of the Bradley outfit had already been blasted out of their saddles.

'There, fellas,' Sam Cranton shouted above the din of gunfire, leading the charge to a shallow dip in the terrain:

poor cover, but the only cover around. But before they reached the dip, two more men were spun from their mounts by the vicious hail of lead.

Crashing into the dip alongside Cranton, Ben Bradley wiped the sweat of fear from his pale face. Having started out with twelve men, not counting the Bradley Creek marshal, he now had six left, reduced to five just as his count recorded six. Their return fire was token, because popping heads up for the couple of seconds it took to take aim invited a bullet between the eyes.

The bandits slowed their approach, savouring the final moment of conquest like a cat toying with an injured bird. Ben Bradley's plea to Cranton was a desperate one.

'What the hell are we going to do, Sam?'

Though the danger of a wipe-out was on the cards, Cranton took time to savour Bradley's cringing. For years he had had to kowtow to the rancher, doing his dirty work and suffering his insults and humiliation. He could have never, in his wildest dreams, have imagined that one day the cock-of-the-hoop Ben Bradley would be pleading for his help.

'Tell me what to do, Sam,' Bradley whined. 'I don't want to die!'

'I don't think that there's much chance of living, Ben,' the Bradley Creek marshal said, calmly turning the screw another notch. 'That honcho on the white stallion is none other than Eduardo Sanchez.'

Knowing well the bandit's blood-soaked history, Ben Bradley's pallor blanched even more.

'But maybe — '

'What?' the rancher begged, his anxiety at its peak and threatening to drive him out of his mind. Sam Cranton looked Bradley squarely in the eye.

'For me to try what I've got in mind, I'll have to stand up and face Sanchez, and that's a mighty big risk, Ben. The kind of risk a man would need a lot of *dinero* to take.'

'Anything, Sam,' Bradley said feverishly.

'Half the ranch,' Cranton stated boldly. 'Me and you equal partners.'

'You're loco!'

'That's the deal, Ben. Take it or leave it,' Cranton stated bluntly.

'You'll die too.'

'I ain't got much to live for,' Cranton said forlornly. 'All I amount to is a falling down clapboard house that the town owns, a new pair of boots and a horse that's losing its wind.' He sat back and took the makings from his pocket. 'Guess it's time for that last smoke, Ben.'

'Agreed,' Bradley snarled. 'We'll draw up the papers as soon as we get back to the ranch.'

Cranton shook his head. 'We'll do that right now, Ben, if you don't mind.'

'Now? How? I ain't got nothing to write with.'

Cranton took a dodger he had stuffed in his pocket, and produced the stub of a pencil. 'One thing about being a marshal, Ben. You've always got to be ready to write things down.' Finished writing on the back of the dodger, he handed the note to Bradley. It read:

Me, Ben Bradley, do this day . . . make Sam Cranton an equal partner in my ranch.

'Fill in the date where I've left the gap, and sign it.'

Glowering, Ben Bradley grudgingly did as Cranton instructed. 'Your plan to get us out of this had better work, Cranton,' he growled, hatred for his former boot-licker glowing in his narrowed eyes.

Cranton smirked. 'It won't matter if it doesn't.' His smirk became a cocky grin. '*Partner*,' he added sarcastically. He called on two men to witness the agreement.

Bradley snorted. 'Don't you trust me, Sam?'

'Like a rattler in my pocket, Ben,' Cranton answered with a chuckle.

Witnessed, he shoved the agreement in his pocket. 'Wish me luck, fellas,' he said, and stood up.

* * *

Jethro Billings burst from the cave. Jack Strother cursed and opened covering fire which, not knowing how many there were or the positions of Sanchez's men, was wholly speculative. He looked in astonishment as the old-timer charged past, headed out of the canyon. Strother's anger at what he saw as Billings's desertion was short-lived, when two bandits high up in the canyon showed in their attempt to bring down the old-timer. It was then that Jethro's plan became clear. He had risked his life in the hope that the bandits would do exactly as they had done — break cover to try and nail him.

Grabbing the opportunity Jethro's daredevil dash had handed him, Jack Strother's rifle exploded. One of the Mexicans grabbed his chest and toppled head-long. The gut-wrenching crack of breaking bones echoed through the canyon as he tumbled down. His fall was silent, which meant that he had been already dead before he pitched off his high perch. The second bandit fled for cover, but not before Strother's second shot wounded him. Clutching his side, he looked done for. And if not fatally wounded, the Mexican was at least much less of a threat.

Glancing back and seeing the sharpness of Strother's shooting, Jethro drew rein.

'Let's get outta here, while we still can, Jack!' he hollered.

Swinging into the saddle, Strother called back.

'You'll not get any argument with me about that, Jethro.'

A short distance along the trail they came upon the bandits' horses, ground-hitched, and accepted the sturdy stallions as the gift they were.

'You think that God might be looking on us kindly, Jack?' Jethro giggled.

'Might be at that Jethro. I guess he's waiting for you to have a bath before he calls you to judgment.'

Jethro sniffed at himself.

'A wise sorta fella, God,' he concluded.

On reaching the opening of the canyon they slowed their pace, reckoning that it would be wiser to creep away rather than engage in foolish bravado.

Joshing Strother, Jethro said: 'Ain't the Western hero supposed to be proud and cock his nose at danger, Jack?'

'I heard something about that,' Strother said. 'But I've always figured that there ain't no pride in high-tailing it with your ass peppered with lead, Jethro.'

'You know, Strother, you might just live long enough to be as old as me.'

Riding along a little while later, Strother said:

'That was a brave and mighty fine thing you did back there in the canyon, Jethro. I thank you.'

'Heck,' the old-timer rumbled, 'when

you get to be as long in the tooth as me, you ain't got much to lose anyways. And besides, I owed you for the stand you took for Ike agin that no-good Ben Bradley.'

Both men exchanged sudden and alarmed glances as the ground beneath them began to shake.

'Tarnation,' Jethro grumbled. 'That's all we need, a damn earth tremor! If not a full-blooded quake!' he added, as the shaking of the ground intensified.

16

Bambridge glanced behind him at her ladyship, one breast tantalizingly exposed, legs whorishly parted, looking every inch a harlot. The transition shocked him, and he wondered if the Lyle-Hackett line was as untainted and pure as they would have one believe.

'Good show, m'lady,' he complimented.

'Eyes ahead, Bambridge,' she commanded.

'Certainly. Begging your pardon, m'lady.' He checked on the bandits. 'Battle stations, m'lady.'

Cecily Lyle-Hackett, draped wantonly across a boulder, clutched the derringer which Bambridge had given her.

★ ★ ★

Marshal Sam Cranton faced Eduardo Sanchez.

'You are a very brave or a very foolish man, *señor*,' the bandit leader said. 'Why should I not shoot you down like the Yanqui dog you are?'

'You won't kill me, *señor*,' Cranton said confidently, 'because if you do you will throw away a share in a fabulous treasure.'

The Mexican's heavy eyebrows knitted together.

'Treasure, *Americano*?' he said lazily.

'Ever hear of Raoul's Treasure?'

The outlaw leader's study of the Bradley Creek lawman was a mixture of pity and disbelief.

'Raoul's Treasure, eh. This is the fabulous treasure you speak of?'

Cranton nodded, aware of the shifting ground under his feet, and he began to think that he would never get to own half of the Bradley ranch. Eduardo Sanchez tapped his forehead with his finger. 'This Raoul's Treasure is the talk of a loco man, *señor*.' He laughed. 'You hear this story from an Apache, yes?' His laughter became uproarious. 'The Apaches, they tell this story to fool the Yanquis. They come looking for this treasure and walk into an Apache trap.' The Mexican's eyes became hooded. 'And now, I kill you, Yanqui.'

'What have you got to lose by finding out if Raoul's Treasure exists or not?' Cranton said, hiding his desperation behind a cocky grin. 'We haven't far to go to find out.'

His curiosity piqued by Sam Cranton's thespian skills, he quizzed, 'You know where this treasure is?'

'Yes,' Cranton lied confidently, sensing Sanchez's conversion.

'You tell Sanchez,' he demanded.

'No,' refused Cranton flatly, gambling that he had not pushed his luck too far.

The Mexican snorted.

'No, *señor*?' he said hollowly.

'No,' Cranton restated, tensing for what must be an inevitable bullet. 'If you kill me, the secret dies with me, Sanchez.'

The Mexican pouted his thick lips.

'You drive a hard bargain, Yanqui. Tell me what you have in mind.'

Figuring that he had averted any immediate danger to his well-being, the Bradley Creek marshal gained in confidence.

'Here's the deal, Sanchez. We join forces as equal partners.'

'Heh, Rodriguez, what you say?' Sanchez asked the mixed-blood man beside him. 'You think we should trust this Yanqui dog?'

Rodriguez shrugged. 'We are in no hurry, Eduardo. That train we plan on robbing is not due for another week.'

'Deal, Yanqui,' said Sanchez.

'Good. I'll go talk to my men and then we'll ride together.' Cranton studied Sanchez. 'We heard shooting, señor?'

'Sanchez chase two gringos. A young one and an old man. The old man, he kill my beloved brother Pablo. I return

169

to the canyon, the gringo bastards vanished by some trickery. Then when I have killed them, we ride together, *mi amigo.*'

Two gringos. One young. One old. Jack Strother and Jethro Billings. Cranton's spirits lifted. If they could only pick up their tracks, he might just save his hide yet and live to ride on Bradley Range. However, if Sanchez killed them, his demise was certain. There was nothing he could do but hope that Strother and the old man had somehow managed to escape from the canyon.

As Cranton walked off to rejoin Ben Bradley, Eduardo Sanchez delivered a chilling warning.

'You try and fool Sanchez, *amigo.* And I will cut out your heart.'

★ ★ ★

Larry Saunders collapsed on to the mound of earth he and Nathan Brandy had feverishly scooped out.

'It's no use, Nathan,' he gasped. He looked into the yawning hole in the ground. 'We must be as close to hell as don't matter. Like I said, that Spanish hobo must have had the second half of the map in his head.

Though fighting admission of his same thoughts, the Bradley Creek sawbones had grudgingly to concede that Saunders was probably right.

'I guess we chose the wrong option, huh?' Saunders said despondently. 'We should have lit out after Strother and the old-timer, and dogged their trail.'

Incensed by a reminder of his foolishness, Nathan Brandy snarled.

'If you hadn't opened your big mouth about a map, that's exactly what I would have done, you dumbhead!'

Reacting, Saunders leapt to his feet.

'I've taken about all the lip I'm going to take from you,' he yelled.

'Is that so,' Brandy flung back. 'Then what're you going to do about it?'

The storekeeper settled his awkwardly slung gunbelt. Some men had a natural gun-gait, but Saunders was not such a man. When he finished settling the gunbelt, it still hung as awkwardly on his rounded, fleshy hips as it had before he had started his elaborate rearranging of it.

On the other hand, Brandy slung a gun in a fashion that, had he chosen to follow a profession other than medicine, would have befitted his making his living by dealing out death with a sixgun. There was no doubt that should Saunders pursue his gripe, he would be the loser. It was a split second away from gunfire, when Brandy shot past Saunders.

'Scared, huh!' the storekeeper taunted, fooling himself that the sawbones had taken fright.

Nathan Brandy was closely examining the ragged remains of a boot poking from a pocket of earth that had collapsed at the side of the hole. Saunders was shaking his head. The doc had gone loco. Brandy's interest was in the heel of the boot, which had not deteriorated relative to the rest of it.

'Give me your knife,' he ordered Saunders.

Caught up in Brandy's excitement, Saunders quickly obliged.

Brandy scraped the heel of the boot and revealed it to be made of steel. He feverishly scrutinized the heel, then, eyes glowing, he used the knife to prise open a tiny latch and slid open the heel to reveal a secret hiding-place in its hollow interior. He gingerly extracted from it a sheet of yellow parchment similar to the parchment on which the first half of the map had been drawn.

'Holy shit!' Saunders swore, dropping to his knees alongside Brandy as he opened the parchment and breathlessly joined it to the parchment they found earlier, to form the complete map of Raoul's Treasure.

After a moment of utter awe Saunders leapt to his feet and began prancing about, shouting:

'We're rich, Nathan. Rich as kings.' But his exuberance was calmed by

Brandy's pained frown as he unfolded and read a second piece of parchment from the heel of the boot.

'What is it?' the storekeeper asked tensely, agonized that the riches he had thought were within his grasp would slip away.

'We need to get hold of the damn diamond Strother has to find the treasure!' Brandy grated.

'But we've got the map.'

'All the map does is tell us where the treasure is. But the diamond pinpoints exactly where it's hidden.' Brandy waved the explanatory note in the air. 'It says here that when we reach Devil's Canyon, we'll see what Raoul called the Trinity of Stones. On the tallest of the stones there's a niche into which the diamond must be inserted. Then, at noon, the reflected light from the diamond reveals where the treasure lies.'

Bereft, Saunders wailed.

'All this for nothing. That damn dago's map is worth tiddly without the

174

diamond. Which we ain't got.'

Nathan Brandy's despondency was short-lived. His mood became doggedly stubborn.

'We're not finished yet, Saunders. All we've got to do is get hold of the diamond.'

'And how do we do that? Seeing that Stother's got it.'

'We'll try and pick up their trail before they reach Devil's Canyon.' His features set grimly. 'Kill Strother and the old-timer. Take the diamond, and Raoul's Treasure is all ours, my friend.'

The store-owner shifted uneasily.

'What is it now?' Brandy impatiently questioned Saunders.

'I don't hold with killing in cold blood, Nathan.'

The Bradley Creek doctor looped a comradely arm round the storekeeper's shoulders.

'I can appreciate that, Larry,' he said, cajolingly. 'And there's no problem. I'll kill them!'

Saunders shook his head. 'Never

thought you had it in you, Nathan.'

Brandy said harshly, 'Neither did I. Every day is full of surprises, my friend.'

'Well, I guess, if you'll do the killing, I'll tag along.'

'Good!'

He, of course, did not tell the storekeeper that once he had the diamond, killing three would be as easy as killing two. Turning away, Nathan Brandy grinned wolfishly. Like he had just said, every day is full of surprises.

* * *

The second man of the trio of Mexican bandits drew rein and watched the strange flying object spinning towards him. He remained intrigued right up to the second that the steel-rimmed bowler-hat cleaved off his head. The rider directly behind the headless man ducked as his partner's head flew past, blood splashing across his face. Bambridge reared up and used the makeshift sling-shot

176

with unerring skill. The rock from the sling-shot smashed against the second bandit's forehead and catapulted him from the saddle. He lay on the ground, dazed. Bambridge lost no time. He picked up a sizeable boulder and dropped it on the Mexican's head to smash his skull.

The bandit to whom he had permitted free passage was, as he had expected, stopped dead in his tracks by Cecily Lyle-Hackett, who lost no time in using the precious seconds of the Mexican's mesmerization to put a bullet between his eyes.

'Good show, m'lady,' Bambridge congratulated, climbing down from his perch.

'Won't those other Mexicans have heard my shot?' she worried.

'I estimate that the derringer's sound will not carry that far, m'lady. Now, I think we should hurry along. We would not want to lose touch with Mr Strother and Mr Billings.'

'They're probably dead,' Cecily Lyle-Hackett said gloomily. 'Those

Mexicans will have killed them, I fear, Bambridge.'

Bambridge shook his head.

'I think not, m'lady. If I were a betting man, my money would be on Mr Strother and the wily Mr Billings giving our Mexican friends the slip.'

'I do hope so, Bambridge,' Lady Lyle-Hackett fretted.

Her worry was not solely for the loss of the treasure. Jack Strother was a man who made her pulse race; a man who had, to her disbelief, attracted her more than any other man she had ever encountered.

⋆ ⋆ ⋆

Riding in the shade of a ridge, Jack Strother and Jethro Billings rode as fast as they could over the trembling earth to open ground, hoping to avoid the rocks and debris spilling off the ridge. One giant boulder forced the hard-riding duo to change course several times, in their attempts to second-guess the direction of the bone-crusher. And the danger was that while they weaved and veered all over the place, the lesser missiles could prove every bit as deadly. Because of the height of the ridge, a pebble falling could fracture a man's skull. And with the ground cracking open under them, there was always the danger of their dropping into a chasm that could be a couple of feet or a darn mile deep. It could also close as fast as it had opened up and bury a man alive.

'Damn it, Jethro,' Strother shouted, 'Let's stop this dancing and head in a straight line. If it's our time, then it's our time, friend.'

Low in the saddle, their mounts bucking, trying to make sense of the earth's jig under their hoofs, they rode full out. Clear of falling rocks, they drew rein and simply sat to outwait the heaving of the ground, praying that they had picked the one spot where the earth would remain firm under them. The whole episode lasted no more than twenty seconds, but every second was a lifetime. As the tremor passed and the ground settled, they began to breathe again. Until, right in front of them a massive hole opened up, and began to widen as the the earth was sucked into the yawning cavern. Strother and Jethro felt the ground slide from under them, dragging them relentlessly with it towards the gigantic grave.

17

Cecily Lyle-Hackett held on fiercely to her manservant Bambridge.

'Remain perfectly still, m'lady,' he urged, and comforted her. 'It will soon pass.'

He had experienced many tremors and a couple of earthquakes in his service to the Empire, and knew that there was little point in running around like a headless chicken, because one could be dashing off into trouble instead of avoiding it. He was inclined to the more philosophical view that somewhere the length of your time was recorded, and if it had run out there was nothing one could do about it.

It was Lady Lyle-Hackett's first experience of an earth tremor, and she hoped that it would be her last. Convinced that she was living her final moments, her mind went back to her childhood and young womanhood at Hackett Hall, and she cursed her papa for the studpidity which had robbed her of her birthright. Was her quest to restore the Lyle-Hackett name and fortune to end far from the lush green fields of Kent where she had grown up?

Unbelievably, the ground began to calm and settle.

'There, you see, m'lady,' the manservant said.

'Is it over, Bambridge?'

'Yes. For now. However, tremors are unpredictable,' he cautioned.

'Bambridge,' Cecily Lyle-Hackett pronounced, 'this will be our last adventure. Win or lose, we're going home to England!'

'Yes,' Bambridge mused, his gaze distant, 'it really is about time we sought out civilized society again, m'lady.'

★ ★ ★

'You crazy bastard!' was Ben Bradley's expostulation at Sam Cranton in response to the marshal's outlining of the deal he had struck with Eduardo Sanchez minutes before. 'That Mexican devil will skin us alive when he finds out that we can't lead him to the treasure.'

'Bluff was the only chip we had,' Cranton stated. 'I don't think Sanchez would be impressed with me throwing myself on his mercy. This way we've bought ourselves time. Who knows what'll happen.'

'I know damn well what will happen!' Bradley grated. 'Our bones will be bleached in this hell-hole, that's what will happen.'

'In that case, *partner*,' Cranton sneered. 'You'd better start praying that we can pick up Strother's trail fast.'

★   ★   ★

Jack Strother and Jethro Billings sat looking into the crater which had almost swallowed them, shaking like the last leaf in a fall storm. The earth gave one last heave, like a man belching after a good meal, and settled.

'You know, Jack,' the old-timer sighed, his grin wide. 'That bucking reminded me of the tattooed French woman I dallied a while with in New Orleans.' His eyes filled with fond memories. 'You know, I might make my way back to Orleans after we find this treasure.'

He glanced slyly at Strother.

'She's got a sister, Jack.'

*　*　*

Nathan Brandy and Larry Saunders pushed their horses to the limit to eat up ground in their quest to reach the vicinity of Devil's Canyon before Strother and Billings.

'I reckon that there will be more than Strother and the old-timer making tracks for that treasure,' was Brandy's view. 'In fact, I reckon that that pile of rocks will get mighty crowded. So what we've got to do is waylay Strother and Billings before they reach Devil's

Canyon, and get that diamond. That way we can beat the others to it. Or just sit pretty until they tire of searching and give up.'

'Waiting in desert heat won't be easy,' Saunders worried.

Brandy's eyes glazed over. 'I'd sit on hell's hob to get my hands on that treasure.'

'These nags are pretty tuckered out,' the storekeeper warned, as Brandy upped the pace again.

A short way on, Nathan Brandy's keen ears picked up the sounds of a camp ahead at a dry creek. He drew rein and dismounted.

'You wait here,' he instructed Saunders, and crept forward.

He could see a man, a woman and a child, a little girl about six years old, grubbing. His heart raced when he saw three fresh horses hitched to a wagon. He watched for a while longer to make sure that they were alone. Satisfied that they were, he made his way back to Saunders.

'A couple with a kid up ahead,' he informed the storekeeper. 'With three fresh horses.'

Saunders looked at their exhausted horses.

'These ain't up to much,' he said. 'Figure they'd trade, with a cash difference?'

'Maybe,' Brandy said, absently. 'But they'd wonder why we've been riding our horses so hard, in country where a man should nurse his horse along. That might make them curious.'

The storekeeper humped his shoulders.

'I don't see how else we're going to get our hands on those horses if we don't parley, Nathan.'

'Tell you what, you wait here while I go and talk.'

'Sure,' Saunders happily agreed, fearing that Nathan Brandy's brooding mood was a symptom of evil rotting his brain. He had never seen a man go bad so quickly. Shortly after, when three shots rang out, Larry Saunders worst fears were confirmed. He ran to the creek, and stopped dead in his tracks when he saw the bodies of a man, a woman and a child. Brandy was unhitching the frightened horses from the wagon, made nervous by the stench of fresh blood.

'You didn't parley much, did you!' Saunders raged.

'There was nothing I could do,' Brandy growled. 'The man wouldn't trade, and we needed the horses fast. Now let's saddle up and ride.'

'Did you have to kill the little girl?' Saunders wailed.

'Well we couldn't take her along. She's better off dead than being alone out here.' He shoved the reins into Saunders' hand. 'What's done is done, Larry.'

'I wanted no part of this. I should damn well kill you, Brandy.'

The doc held Saunders' gaze.

'You're part of it now. And no one is going to believe that you weren't.' He let that fact sink into the storekeeper's befuddled brain, and when the truth of what he had said sank in, he added: 'Let's go get that treasure, Larry.'

★　★　★

'Won't be long now,' Jethro told Strother. 'Another hour or so and we'll be in Devil's Canyon, partner.'

Jack Strother's sigh was a weary one.

'Then all we've got to do is find the treasure.'

'Well, maybe it'll just be waiting for us, Jack,' the old-timer said dreamily. 'All that gold and glittering jewels.'

'And maybe we should just turn tail and be satisfied with the diamond, Jethro.'

Jethro did not even consider Strother's proposition. 'Nah, Jack. You know what's even more exciting than finding Raoul's Treasure — hunting for it.'

Strother glanced back again to the rising dust behind them.

'Sanchez, you figure?' Billings asked. Strother nodded. The old-timer spat out a long stream of tobacco juice. 'Persistent Mex bastard. Should've cut his throat when I slit his brother's. They were sleeping side by side.'

'Why did you kill Sanchez's brother, anyway?' Strother wanted to know.

'Because of the way he used a girl. No more than a child, she was.' Jethro let loose another spew of tobacco juice. 'Deserved killing.'

'That he did, my friend,' Jack Strother agreed.

★   ★   ★

Sam Cranton had luck on his side. A short time after joining forces with Sanchez, he picked up sign, and was soon tracking Strother. Though Sanchez was aware of Cranton's lies when he had told him that he knew where the treasure was, he was happy for now to go along with him. If there was no treasure, he would take his pleasure from killing the gringos, especially the old man who had temporarily escaped his wrath. He would pay a terrible price for killing his brother Pablo.

★ ★ ★

An excellent tracker, a craft learned in the service of the British Empire, Bambridge was the closest to Strother and Billings. He lent his spyglass to her ladyship to observe the duo.

'Well done, Bambridge,' Lady Lyle-Hackett complimented the manservant.

'Glad to be of service, m'lady.'

Receiving back the spyglass, he studied the large band of riders east of where Strother was. He recognized the rancher Ben Bradley and Cranton, the marshal of Bradley Creek. The Mexican bandits had joined forces with the rancher's men.

He also saw two other riders, even closer to Strother and Billings, Bradley Creek's doctor and another man whom he did not recognize.

It was, he concluded, getting very crowded indeed.

190

18

It was nearing dusk when they reached Devil's Canyon. Jethro suggested that they should camp outside the canyon until sun-up.

'Ghosts,' he explained, when Strother was taken aback.

'Ghosts!' Jack Strother exclaimed, scepticism showing in every sun-seared facial wrinkle. He was about to laugh until he saw how serious and scared the old-timer was. 'Yeah. Ain't no point in rushing in when it's getting dark,' he said kindly.

'You don't believe me, do you, Strother?' the old man groused. 'But it's true. That damn canyon is full of spirits. I heard stories about men going in there as healthy as a buck, and they come out loco to the day they died. Steal your senses, they do. Your soul, too.'

Jethro's gullibility surprised Strother. For a sharp ace of a fella, he had fallen for the oldest ruse in the West. When someone wanted to protect what they had, they did it by circulating a tall yarn about ghosts and curses. And it worked most times, because the West was a raw country, as new as a pin to whitemen who were wary of the pagan worship of the Indians. A land that was a mix of myth, legend, hearsay and rumour. Where a whisper of a strange happening soon took on all sorts of weird connotations. And before you knew it, the howl of a coyote became the moaning of the devil, and a curl of evening dew became a ghostly spectre.

'You think that I'm just a crazy old fool, don't you?' The old man challenged Strother. 'Well, if you're so surefire certain that there ain't no ghosts in that canyon, you go camp there. On your darn own!'

'Don't take on so, Jethro,' Strother said. 'I ain't giving you any argument. If you say there're ghosts in that canyon,

192

then there're ghosts in that damn canyon.'

'Scared, ain't you,' Jethro sneered.

'I ain't scared,' Strother emphasized.

'Ya are, too,' the old-timer taunted.

'Will it be an end of this if I say I'm scared?'

'Might be.'

'Then I'm shivering in my boots, Jethro. OK?'

'OK,' the old man said. 'No need to get your dander up.'

Strother was about to respond, but knew that if he wanted the disagreement to end, it would only do so if Jethro Billings got his own way, stubborn old mule that he was. So he buttoned his lip.

They pitched camp in a circle of stunted trees, parched and twisted into ugliness by the desert sun. Having left Bradley Creek without supplies, jerky and water had been their every meal. Jethro looked with distaste at the unappetizing fare and sighed dreamily.

'First thing I'm going to do when I

get my hands on Raoul's Treasure is head for Abbéville, and get me a thick juicy steak with all the trimmings, Jack, at that fancy hotel they've got there. After, I'll mosey along to the Crooked Dime saloon, get me one of Art Baker's doves, not young and pretty, buxom and big-butted. I'll take her to the biggest feather bed Art's got. Then I'll order his best bottle of rye, lie back, and probably die of sheer pleasure.'

Both men laughed heartily at the scenario the old-timer had painted.

'What're you going to do with your half, Jack?'

'Buy a pretty Montana Valley I came across a couple of years ago. And build the finest herd of beef a man can build, Jethro.'

'You want to nurse cows!' Jethro shook his head in wonder, his craggy jaws shaking. 'That ain't no fit ambition for a man who'll be stinking rich.'

Their reminiscing was cut short by the skitter of a disturbed pebble.

'Easy, Jethro,' Strother murmured.

'Might just be a night creature.'

'Don't figure so,' Jethro opined, in a whisper.

*   *   *

Nathan Brandy cursed silently. The roll of the tiny pebble dislodged by his boot sounded as loud as the clanging of a town fire-bell at midnight. Larry Saunders took advantage of the pause to plead his case for negotiation with Strother and Billings, instead of murder.

'Ain't no call for no more killing, Nathan,' he pleaded. 'I figure we can strike a deal with Strother and the old man. They've got the diamond, sure enough. But they don't know how to use it to pinpoint the treasure without us telling them.'

'That'll mean a fourway split,' Brandy grumbled.

'If this Raoul's Treasure exists, we'll still all be rich.'

'But not as rich if we only halved the treasure,' the Bradley Creek sawbones cajoled, confident that greed would persuade Saunders to go along with his skulduggery.

However, Saunders remained steadfast in his opposition to more killing. Brandy seemed to relent.

'I guess you're right, Larry. Lead the way, and we'll talk with Strother and Billings, as you want to.'

The storekeeper beamed. 'You'll see,' he said. 'They'll see sense, Nathan.'

Brandy stepped aside to allow Saunders to go ahead. He picked up a rock and smashed the storekeeper's skull. He smiled evilly, his eyes wild with madness.

'Now I get the whole pie, partner.'

* * *

In the gloaming, Bambridge could see the lone figure creeping towards Strother and Billings's camp, and a skulking figure could only have one purpose — mischief, and probably of a deadly kind.

'Shouldn't we do something, Bambridge?' Lady Lyle-Hackett said.

'I shouldn't think so, m'lady,' he opined. 'I *reckon*,' Cecily Lyle-Hackett looked in alarm on hearing Bambridge's Americanism, delivered with the diction and accent of a rough-house cowboy, 'Mr Strother is well capable of taking care of himself.' He had mischievously thought about adding *ma'am*. But considered the additional shock might be too much for her ladyship to bear.

For her part, she vowed to make every effort to get Bambridge back to England before his language and demeanour were totally corrupted.

'I respectfully suggest, m'lady, that we await the outcome of the impending fracas, before we initiate any action of our own.'

'But I fear for Jack's safety, Bambridge,' Cecily Lyle-Hackett fretted.

Jack!

Oh, dear, the manservant thought, he would have to do everything in his power to repatriate her ladyship to the civilized shores of England as soon as possible. Could it be possible that her ladyship was so taken with the rough-and-ready Westerner, to be considering a liaison? If not a relationship of a more permanent nature. If such came to pass, he would be the first in a long family line of retainers to the Lyle-Hacketts to fail so disastrously and so spectacularly in his duty to, at all times, steer their employers and their offspring away from situations which might be fraught with the kind of complications any association with the lower classes inevitably would have.

'As I opined, m'lady,' Bambridge intoned, with the traditional down-the-nose-look which English servants used to convey their disapproval to their masters and mistresses, 'I dare say that Mr Strother' — his pause was utter perfection — '*Jack*, is more than capable of seeing off any threat to his person.'

Lady Cecily Lyle-Hackett, coached

from an early age to avoid upsetting the servants, disregarded that comment.

'You know, Bambridge' she said boldly, 'there may come a time when Mr Strother will be your master.'

Good God! Were that to happen, suicide would become an attractive option. However, with the unquestioning obedience instilled in him from the cradle Bambridge appeared unmoved.

'I am, of course, always ready to accommodate your ladyship's wishes and domestic arrangements,' he said.

'I never doubted your diligence and loyalty, Bambridge,' she said.

'That scoundrel is rather close to Mr Strother now, m'lady,' Bambridge said. 'We must hope for a pleasing outcome.'

'We must indeed, Bambridge,' Cecily Lyle-Hackett said fervently.

* * *

'All we've got to do is sit tight,' Sam Cranton told Eduardo Sanchez, hoping to stymie the Mexican bandit's natural instincts to charge in. 'Why risk our hides? When they find the treasure we can easily snatch it from them.'

'We will wait,' Sanchez decided, after a short consideration of Cranton's proposal. 'But not for too long, *mi amigo*,' he warned.

The Bradley Creek marshal reported back to Ben Bradley on the outcome of his discussion with the bandit leader, much to the rancher's relief. But not to the point where he could relax completely, seeing Cranton's success more as a temporary respite from the danger that haunted every second of their association with the explosive Mexican.

'I sure hope that Raoul's Treasure is not a yarn, Cranton,' Bradley worried. 'Because if it is, that damn canyon is going to be our graveyard.'

It was a worry shared. But setting his worries firmly aside, Sam Cranton remained upbeat.

'Sure it'll be there, Ben.' He dared not contemplate otherwise, now that he had secured what he had always wanted as Bradley's partner — range and cows. They could keep Raoul's Treasure, he already had his.

Holding on to it would be the problem.

*   *   *

On Jack Strother's urging, they continued with their camp-fire banter about what they would do once they got their hands on the treasure, appearing to remain oblivious to Nathan Brandy's lurking presence, and resisting the urge to take pre-emptive action. Strother knew that the timing of his response to the impending threat would be all important. Act a second too soon, and he would lose the advantage of surprise. Leave it a second too long, and it would be a second too late.

Brandy was encouraged by what he perceived as Strother's and the old-timer's unawareness of him. Not having proficiency with his recently acquired sixgun, it was necessary for him to get close to his victims to be certain that his first shots would kill them, or at least maim them sufficiently to remove any threat of retaliation.

Just a couple of feet more, and he'd be ready to shoot.

19

Jack Strother spun round in the same second that Nathan Brandy drew a bead on his back, the trigger of the .45 within a hair's breath of exploding the Colt. His judgement was inch-perfect; his pistol clearing leather in a blink.

'Drop it!' he barked.

Brandy's fevered brain was slow to react, too slow to prevent Strother's sixgun from blasting. Nathan Brandy staggered back, looking at the ragged hole in his gut. In a reflex action, his finger triggered his gun. The discharged load buzzed past Jack Strother, uncomfortably close. He spun around in alarm on hearing Jethro's yelp, in time to see the old-timer's hat coming back down, still spinning in the air.

'God damn it, Jack,' Jethro swore, poking his fist through the holed crown of the ancient and grubby headgear. 'I was saving this hat for my funeral.'

Strother chuckled. 'If that bullet was a smidgen lower, you'd have got to use it while it's still even half-decent.'

'What's that *hombre* clutching?'

When Strother glanced back, he saw the yellowed parchment in Brandy's grasp. The doc's fading eyes held an ocean of regret as they closed.

Jethro rushed past Strother, having no qualms about relieving the dead man of the bloodied parchment.

'It's a darn map,' he said excitedly. 'Got a lot of writing. Can you read?' he enquired of Strother anxiously.

'Some.'

Jethro handed the parchment with the explanation of the diamond's importance in discovering the exact whereabouts of Raoul's Treasure to Strother.

'Well, what's it say?' the old-timer impatiently pressed his partner, as Jack Strother's jaw dropped. When he informed Jethro of the parchment's contents and instructions the old man gulped, and his eyes widened in marvel.

'I'll be damned, Jack,' he murmured. Then, chuckling, added: 'At least there's a good chance I will be now.'

★ ★ ★

In their not too distant hidy-hole, observing Strother and Billings prancing about, Bambridge told Lady Lyle-Hackett: 'It seems, m'lady, that Mr Strother and Mr Billings have received good tidings. And I would go so far as to say that it is imperative that we discuss what should be done to acquire Raoul's Treasure, once it is discovered. For it is my firm belief, m'lady, that the good tidings Mr Strother and Mr Billings have received is the last piece of the jigsaw to unlock Raoul's secret.'

'You would say, Bambridge?' Cecily Lyle-Hackett said breathlessly.

'I would, m'lady.'

'Then Raoul's Treasure really exists?' she said in awe.

'That is my conclusion, m'lady,'

Bambridge said.

Lady Lyle-Hackett recovered her composure, which Bambridge thought had rather distressingly slipped.

'We will, of course, do whatever is necessary to make the treasure ours, Bambridge,' she said.

'Good show, m'lady,' the manservant beamed.

★　★　★

There were other observers of Strother's and Billings's delighted jig, and the Sanchez and Bradley combination reached the same conclusion as the English aristocrat and her manservant. They shared the common goal of acquiring Raoul's Treasure by whatever means necessary.

★　★　★

After the celebration of their good fortune, Jack Strother began to ponder on the problems of holding on to the treasure, once they found it. He was certain that the Bradley Creek saw-bones was only one of many predators, equal in ambition and ruthlessness.

The morrow was going to be an eventful day, with no guarantee that sunset would be seen.

20

At sun-up, Jack Strother and Jethro Billings rode into Devil's Canyon, conscious of the powder-keg of danger that could explode at any second. In the calm of the morning, Jethro briefly doubted Strother's assertion that keeping Raoul's Treasure, once they got their hands on it, would be the devil's own task. But on seeing a puff of dust followed by a handful of shale sliding down from higher up in the canyon, his doubt was no more.

'Maybe we should just ride away from here, friend,' Strother suggested, before riding deeper into the canyon. 'Treasure ain't any good to a dead man.'

Jethro considered Strother's proposal, but decided against it.

'You go if you want, Jack. Leave the diamond. If I get outta here, I'll see that you get it back.'

Jack Strother handed over the diamond.

'Always figured it was yours anyway, Jethro.'

A while later, as Strother continued to ride alongside, the old-timer spoke up.

'I thought you were riding out.'

'No,' Strother confirmed. 'I figure that having started together, we'll end together. If that's OK with you, partner?'

Jethro smiled. 'Just dandy, friend.'

'Then,' Jack Strother sighed, 'let's find that Trinity of Stones this *hombre* Raoul talks about, and find his treasure.'

It took most of the morning to find the three rocks jutting out at the base of a steep rockface.

'Trinity, I guess,' he said. They headed straight for the stones, not bothered about any trackers, because there was little they could do about their presence. Jethro took the diamond from his pocket and placed it in the hole on top of the tallest of the three stones, as per Raoul's instructions.

'Fits perfectly,' he said. 'Now we wait, Jack?'

The noon sun poked through a narrow crevice high up in the canyon. The diamond dazzled. As the sun moved across the fissure the shaft of light became concentrated and drew a line in the opposite rockface, highlighting what looked like a crack in its surface. But its line was way too perfect for nature to have drawn it.

'Quickly,' Strother urged Jethro. 'Once the sun passes, that opening in the rockface will vanish.'

He ran to the rockface, where he saw that there was room for a man's fingers to grab at the slim edge of an opening. He pulled hard.

'Help me, Jethro.'

The old-timer joined Strother in what seemed to him to be a loco task, trying to tear a rockface apart. However, to his utter amazement there was a deep rumble from within the rockface, and it began to open, the heavy door of rock rolling back on an elaborate mechanism of different sized boulders. As the two men held their breath the man-made cavern, hewn from the rockface, revealed several steelbanded caskets. Jethro quickly overcame his wonder. He stepped inside the small cave and took a rock to break open the lock of one of the caskets. Treasure beyond his wildest dreams glistened inside it. Diamonds. Rubies. Emeralds. Gold.

'There must be at least a dozen caskets, Jack,' he croaked.

Their contemplation of their enormous riches, was cut short by the cocking of a gun. Strother and Jethro swung around. Bambridge, accompanied by Cecily Lyle-Hackett filled the entrance of the cave.

'I won't hesitate to kill you, Jack,' she said, 'if that's what it takes. But, frankly,' her gaze ran over the caskets, 'I think there's more than enough for all, don't you?'

'It would be wise to accept her ladyship's generous offer, gentlemen,' Bambridge said.

'It ain't that easy a decision, friend,' Jack Strother said, looking beyond the English duo.

More guns were cocked.

'It sure as hell is crowded round here, Jack,' Jethro Billings groused, as the Sanchez and Bradley men crowded the entrance to the Aladdin's cave.

'If you'll just step outside, *señors* and *señorita*,' Sanchez invited. 'My men will take my treasure.'

'*Your* treasure,' Ben Bradley barked. 'Now just wait a sec — '

The Mexican's gun blasted, cutting down Ben Bradley. It was the cue for the entire bandit gang to open up. Seconds later, not a Bradley man was left standing. Sanchez's attention now switched to Cecily Lyle-Hackett, his hooded eyes smouldering with lust.

'You will ride with Eduardo Sanchez,' he told her.

'Don't be bloody silly, you greasy

dago!' she exploded.

'Now look here, my good man . . . '

Sanchez raked his gun barrel across Bambridge's left cheek.

'Speak again and I will cut your tongue out,' the Mexican promised. He took Bambridge's bowler-hat and put it on his head, much to the amusement of the bandits.

'Mex bastard!' Jethro growled. 'Knew I should've killed you with your brother, when I had the chance.'

Sanchez looked with scorn on the old-timer.

'You I will kill slowly, old man.' His gaze settled on Jack Strother. 'You, I will give a choice, señor. Die here, or ride with Eduardo Sanchez.'

'I couldn't stand your stink, Sanchez,' Strother said.

Sanchez laughed. 'You are a fool, señor. But first, the treasure. Pronto,' he shouted, herding his men inside the cave. 'I will stand guard.'

Seconds after entering the cave, the ground shook and heaved. The earth tremor split the rockface and it crumbled, collapsing in on itself. The canyon was filled with the screams of the men trapped inside the cave. The earth split open to swallow the cave and bury the men alive.

Jethro was first to overcome his surprise. Seizing his chance to complete what he reckoned he should have completed before, he grabbed a knife from Ben Bradley's boot and with a deft flick, sank it in Eduardo Sanchez's throat.

Clutching at the knife, the bandit leader staggered back, teetering on the brink of the gigantic hole which had opened up. He got off a wild shot before pitching into it. Another great heave and the hole closed.

The earth stopped moving.

Raoul's Treasure had vanished into the bowels of the earth.

When the cloud of dust settled Jack Strother, trying to figure out why Jethro Billings wasn't crowing, sought him. The bandit's wild shot had caught

Jethro square in the chest. Strother hurried to the dying man's side.

'The diamond's in my right trousers pocket,' he gaspingly told Strother. 'And I don't want no fool talk about it not being rightly yours.' He grinned, but the light was leaving his eyes. 'So long, partner,' he croaked, and lay still.

When the heavy silence of mourning eased, Jack Strother held out the diamond in the palm of his hand.

'I figure that Jethro would want you to share in this, Cecily,' he said.

'There's only one way I would share it, Jack,' she said fondly.

★   ★   ★

'What did he call me?' Lady Bessingham, a friend of Cecily Lyle-Hackett exclaimed. 'A filly! I feel quite, quite faint.'

'And what are these *steers* he keeps talking about?' another woman nearby wondered.

'And longhorns, too,' another said.

215

'What kind of creatures are they?'

Jack Strother had passed on through the french windows to the garden of Hackett Hall, anxious to leave the soirée behind. He looked out on the perfectly manicured lawns that were as far removed from prairie grass as the moon was from earth. He sniffed the air; it was scented, not a speck of prairie dust in it.

It had been a year since Cecily and he had arrived back in England to reclaim Hackett Hall; a year in which he had begun to yearn for real beer and wide open spaces that went on unbroken by neatly trimmed boundaries that divided the land up into sections, and destroyed the way nature intended it to be.

'Not a cactus in sight, Jack.'

He turned to greet Cecily, now Mrs Jack Strother.

'Nor a creek or water-hole either.' Strother sighed, and slid his arm round his wife's waist. 'And none of those golden sunsets that go on for ever.'

They remained looking out over the lush Kent countryside, as the hunt vanished over a distant crest. Then Cecily called out.

'Bambridge!'

The manservant appeared as if by magic.

'Your ladyship?'

'Pack what we need for passage to America,' she said.

'America, m'lady?' he asked, stunned.

'Yes, Bambridge. Mr Strother and I are going home.'

★ ★ ★

Jack Strother looked over the Montana valley he had dreamed of every night since he had first set eyes on it, and sat his horse contentedly.

'You'll have to teach me all about ranching, darling,' Cecily Strother said.

He looked at her bulging tummy.

'In time,' he said. 'In time, woman.'

'If it's a boy we'll call him Jethro,' she said.

'That will please me mightily, Cecily,' Jack Strother said.

Bambridge came riding towards them, dressed as he would have been in Hackett Hall. He drew rein and brushed the dust from his clothing.

'Afternoon tea is served, ma'am,' he intoned.

He rode back down the hill, shaking his head.

Cecily Strother laughed. 'You know, Jack, one day we English will civilize this country,' she said.

'God forbid!' Jack Strother yelped. 'Beat you back to the house, wife!'

Jack and Cecily Strother galloped helter-skelter down the hill past Bambridge with wild yells, scattering cows in all directions. As he watched them into the distance, the manservant observed whimsically:

'Not at all like the Boxing Day Hunt, ma'am.'